Days

of

Rage

Cas Dunlap

ALSO BY CAS DUNLAP
Southern Lights
It's News to Us
Beach Breezes
The Casa Linda Chronicles: Short Stories and Stuff
The Process
Celestial Blues
To Kill an Angel
Flock 'Em!
Beach Karma

First Edition

Anegada Press
Pensacola Beach, Florida

Printed in the United States of America

Library of Congress Control Number 2013949946

ISBN: 978-0-9670420-9-1

DEDICATION

To my brothers and sisters of the quill who have transcended the great divide and who now know "who done it" in life's greatest mystery. We mortals miss you.

ACKNOWLEDGMENTS

Normally this part includes several paragraphs of thanks to the people who have helped get a book written. This time it's a pretty short list: Anne, who is my wife and editor, and me. That's it. My part is what it is and I enjoyed every bit of it. Anne's part is more tedious and difficult and my gratitude to her is beyond description.

Do not go gentle into that good night

Do not go gentle into that good night,
Old age should burn and rave at close of day;
Rage, rage against the dying of the light.

Though wise men at their end know dark is right,
Because their words had forked no lightning they
Do not go gentle into that good night.

Good men, the last wave by, crying how bright
Their frail deeds might have danced in a green bay,
Rage, rage against the dying of the light.

Wild men who caught and sang the sun in flight,
And learn, too late, they grieved it on its way,
Do not go gentle into that good night.

Grave men, near death, who see with blinding sight
Blind eyes could blaze like meteors and be gay,
Rage, rage against the dying of the light.

And you, my father, there on the sad height,
Curse, bless, me now with your fierce tears, I pray.
Do not go gentle into that good night.
Rage, rage against the dying of the light.

— Dylan Thomas

Contents

Days

of

Rage

RAGE, RAGE

Sitting here immobilized, in pain, I don't have much to do except ruminate about how this situation came to be. I mean, all the good-looking lady newscasters on Fox are finished for the day and, until the heavy hitters take over in late afternoon and evening, all that's on is some crazy person who even makes "wingnuts" sound sane.

I wonder if Fox TV took its name because of the number of drop-dead gorgeous women it employs to parrot the news. But now I've strayed way off the point.

So let me start with some simple background. First, I'm a sixty-five-year-old guy who does not golf. And I retired a few years ago for some reason. Now I'm not sure why, but I think Jimmy Buffett had something to do with it. Singing about sunshine and beach drinks and partying around without a care in the world by the placid sea while bikini-clad women sunned.

Yeah. That sounded good on weekends when I knew that "sure as wind blow and grass grow" Monday would start around five in the morning and be followed by endless days of boredom alternating with panic. I had been at my job for years and could do it in my sleep – in fact sometimes I did, I'm pretty sure. But then something would go kerflooey and all hell would break loose as the fate of the company depended on getting something done yesterday – my job to fix it.

Perhaps it was the aging process that caused me to think that I could retire to an idyllic life and live my "golden years" (I hate that term) in bliss.

Anyway, after consulting with my reason-for-living (*aka* my wife) and calculating and re-calculating our resources, I hung up my spurs, so to speak, and we headed for the beach.

Well, at first it was pretty sweet. We found a place by the ocean. The warm sun baked our fish-belly-white hides until they were a more attractive shade of brown. Whenever I woke up, I got to read the newspaper from front to back sitting on my balcony fanned by light sea breezes. Fresh fish for dinner. Lots and lots of beer. Life was good.

The problem was, after a few months, I got bored. I was turning into a brain-dead old fat brown alcoholic. Life was good after the fashion of a cow contentedly munching its cud and staring listlessly off in the distance at nothing in particular.

It was then that I began to get cranky, which made me hard to live with. Recognizing the dilemma, my reason-for-living began to make helpful little suggestions as to what I might do to occupy myself. I think she did this because she's a sweetie-pie, but mainly because she grew sick of having to put up with an old fat bald curmudgeon all the time – even if he *was* brown.

At first all these "little suggestions" were irritating, but after I had a chance to think it through, I didn't blame her and resolved to try to find something to keep me from drifting off into space while bitching about it.

And that's when it happened. She suggested we go out to a poetry reading.

Let me say right up front, I'm not much on poetry.

Maybe a limerick or something that rhymes, but nothing heavy-duty. Under normal circumstances, I sure wouldn't pass up evening cocktails to go hear a poetry recitation. However, I had made the commitment to try, so one evening, off we went to the library.

You can believe I went wild with excitement at the prospect of sitting through the collected works of Percy Nightengale as read by Prudence Plumblossom. On the other hand, there would be wine and light *hors d'oeuvres* for the social hour preceding the main event. Backsliding on my commitment, I wondered if I could sleep through the Percy and Prudence show if I drank enough wine.

What I had been expecting was a bunch of old beatniks dressed in black, capped with black berets, and snapping their fingers for applause. Actually, a few did fit that mold, but, not counting a few kids, most of the people pretty much looked like me and Sweetie Pie. They all seemed to be into wine. How bad could they be?

It turned out that Prudence Plumblossom was an attractive lady of about my age whose real name was Sissy. And instead of Percy, the entrée was Dylan Thomas. I didn't know Sissy, but Dylan had been a friend of mine in high-school

English. Of course, we had grown apart over time. So I couldn't remember anything he had written. But at least the name was familiar.

Sissy began to read and I was immediately transported to another realm of consciousness. That is to say, I didn't remember anything about Dylan Thomas and was fast being put to sleep by Sissy's soft voice.

It could have been destiny, but it was more likely Sweetie Pie's sharp elbow that caused me to come back to full consciousness just as Sissy began her reading of *Do not go gentle into that good night*:

Do not go gentle into that good night,
Old age should burn and rave at close of day;
Rage, rage against the dying of the light.

Though wise men at their end know dark is right,
Because their words had forked no lightning they
Do not go gentle into that good night.

Good men, the last wave by, crying how bright
Their frail deeds might have danced in a green bay,
Rage, rage against the dying of the light.

Wild men who caught and sang the sun in flight,
And learn, too late, they grieved it on its way,
Do not go gentle into that good night.

Grave men, near death, who see with blinding sight
Blind eyes could blaze like meteors and be gay,
Rage, rage against the dying of the light.

And you, my father, there on the sad height,
Curse, bless, me now with your fierce tears, I pray.
Do not go gentle into that good night.
Rage, rage against the dying of the light.

Of course, I couldn't get all the meaning – if there was some more – but the poet's words rang clear when he implored "do not go gentle into that good night… rage, rage against the dying of the light."

I immediately translated that into twenty-first-century speak: don't just sit there watching Fox News until you begin to drool and get sent off to the old folks holding-facility for lingering death. Get into what's left of your life and live every bit of juice out of it until the grim reaper drags you kicking and screaming into the void – or something like that.

I began wondering. *Hey, why didn't I think of that? Why is it necessary to follow old bromides like "act your age" or "grow old gracefully" and "put away something for the kids"? Why should I care if other people think I'm not acting my age or growing old gracefully? They're not paying my bills, and one minute after I'm dead, I personally won't care what any human thinks. And the kids? It's about time they made their own.*

Talk about your shining moment of insight. I must have muttered something because I got the elbow again, and when I looked, Sweetie Pie was giving me the please-don't-embarrass-me look.

I shrugged and fell back on the lessons I had learned in college that had carried me so well through the world of business meetings. I feigned rapt attention while wandering off into my personal world of fantasy.

So there I had it. Who knew how much longer I had to live? But however long it was, I would live it with gusto. I would indeed rage against the dying of the light.

As the applause began at Sissy's conclusion, something occurred to me. *Just how does one rage?*

On the trip back to the beach, I explained my revelation to Sweetie Pie. She seemed pleased, commenting, "That's nice, dear." However, I didn't let her patronizing attitude slow me down; later that night, the sleep that came so easily at the reading evaded me as I tried to decide how I might go about raging.

I guess it finally came down to what I would really like to do that would not get me into serious trouble. Armed with that guideline, I immediately discarded a solo trip to Las Vegas. However, the more I thought, the wearier I got, and the more sitting in front of the TV sounded like something I'd really like to do. In fact, the whole idea of launching out on some adventure began to sound a little scary and just a bit too much effort.

The next thing I knew, I was staring at my sun-lighted ceiling as the events of the prior night regenerated. Rather than lie in bed thinking about raging and its limitations – an unusual activity that I was fairly sure Sweetie Pie would find suspect – I opted to put the whole thing out of my mind until after coffee and my newspaper.

One of the things a beach is really good for is walking on while contemplating stuff. So when Sweetie Pie headed out for the grocery store, I headed out for the beach and a long contemplative stroll.

The bikini-clad chicklets frolicking here and there were distracting, but I resolved to focus on the problem. And while it immediately became clear that I had been on the right track last night, I had failed to reckon on a major stumbling block. Finding something that I really wanted to do was the first part of raging, but the second part was generating the verve and nerve to actually do it. This second part was something that had never occurred to me. I was growing old and the energy, perhaps libido, that is part of youth was waning. That and, almost by definition, the youthful attitude of immortality and invulnerability was tempered with a large dose of reality that comes with the experience of life.

For better or worse, the second part of raging seemed to strongly influence the first part. For instance, once upon a time staying out partying most of the night seemed like great fun. Now, if it doesn't happen by ten o'clock, I don't have the energy. Plus I understand the perils of life beyond the witching hour. So late-night partying just doesn't have the same attraction it used to; it doesn't *seem* like fun – even if it really might be.

So the dilemma: I wanted to rage, but I wasn't sure I had the energy to rage or the capacity to decide how to rage. Fundamentally, I guess another ol' Brit phrased it best: "To be or not to be?" I was loosely defining "not being," but it would include sitting in front of the TV drooling over Fox's foxes.

The whole conundrum became depressing. Fortunately, the beach came to my rescue. On my walk home, I noted the chicklets again, and it struck me how much energy they seemed to have. And it occurred to me that part of their energy was the result of the activity of expending that energy. Put another way, the more energy they expended, the better condition they were in to expend energy. They were in good shape. (No pun intended.)

So there was my answer. The first step in raging was to get in better physical shape. Then I could more honestly decide, and have the capacity to carry out, my mission to suck every last bit of fun out of life before it was over. Not only that, but in the process I would lose my gut and steel my now-flabby muscles. Who knew? Maybe I would grow hair on my head.

Sweetie Pie decided I had become senile during her trip to the grocery store when she found me in the garage busily making repairs on my old road bike.

"What are you doing?" she said.

"I'm going to start exercising," I said. I figured she could see what I was doing.

A puzzled look spread over her pretty face. "Oh. That's nice, dear."

After an hour, one blown-out tire, and a trip to the

bike shop, I was pretty much covered in grease. But the bike was ready to ride, and I decided to launch on the morrow with the rising sun. I would ride to the other end of our barrier island and back, letting my body dictate my speed. I was psyched, but wise enough not to push my limits.

As luck would have it, the next morning the sun didn't rise. Actually it really did, but it did so behind a mammoth cloudbank. As a result, sunshine did not stream into my room at six-thirty and my big brown eyes did not open until around eight. Something about beach-walking and bike-fixing had worn me out.

I was not deterred, though. The only real problem with a late start was there'd be more traffic on the recreation path. That, and riding at eight o'clock on a cloudy day wasn't nearly as romantic as riding as the sun rose. I skipped my coffee and newspaper, and drank some orange juice instead. Sweetie Pie looked at me funny as I waved a jaunty *adios*.

It had been a few years since I had ridden my bike, but like they say, "Once you learn to ride a bike, you never forget." What they don't mention is that they're talking about the mechanics – as opposed to the skill level.

Imagine a drunken butterfly. That would come close

to describing my efforts as I tried again and again to clip my shoes into the pedals. Finally I was securely locked in and making progress in a straight line. The feel of the wind and sun on my skin was exhilarating. I had surely found the magic fountain and I drank deeply. I could almost feel my youth returning. I was beginning to rage, I think.

Up ahead, I could see what appeared to be a family of distracted beach waddlers. The great white patriarch, sporting long black socks and sandals, was burdened with coolers and beach toys. His equally rotund spouse dragged a screaming child. And an older child, perhaps a teenager, was attached at the ears to something electronic. Their general direction was along the recreation path. Their specific progress seemed to be in all directions, simultaneously moving randomly here and there between abrupt stops to exchange words and make adjustments to clothes and things carried.

This was not good news for any cyclist – it was like a soldier approaching an uncharted minefield. I knew that no matter how loudly I signaled my approach, barring a miracle, they would pay no heed. They were on vacation under the aegis of the gods and the world was theirs exclusively. My only hope was that they would reach whatever beach cutoff they sought and waddle off the recreation path before I got there. That didn't seem to be happening.

When I reached what I thought might be within shouting distance, I began to alert them to my approach. "Yo. Bike coming. Watch out. Passing on your left. Move. Hey. Wake up."

Then the miracle happened. Dad somehow saw my bike bearing down and began to herd his brood from the path. I breathed a sigh of relief, slowed, and hugged the side of the path they had vacated.

But just as I almost cleared the herd, the teenager said, "Dad, I forgot my…" and turned directly into my path.

There was nothing I could do. I hit the brakes hard and began to ineffectually jerk at my securely clipped feet. Of course, because I was out of practice and because the clip-on pedals were the one thing I had neglected to oil and check, the pegs did not move from the pedals, the shoes did not move from the pegs, and my foot did not move from my shoes as I began my trip toward the asphalt in slow motion.

Obviously, this event could not really happen in slow motion, so there was no time to consider how I might best land to minimize the damage to my body. My right shoulder took the whole impact.

So that's how I came to be sitting here painfully reliving my attempt at raging against that good night. The fall on my shoulder resulted in a torn rotator cuff. I'll spare you the details, but if you've ever had one, you know. Six weeks in a sling. Six months of rehab. And naturally it was my good right arm that was damaged. Think that through, if you dare.

It turns out that the waddlers were nice people. They called an ambulance and waited until it arrived before they wandered off toward the beach.

And my raging against the good night? I haven't given up. I still don't intend to go gently. The process has just been put on a six-month hold. Then I think I'll start out with something a little more manageable. Perhaps, instead of raging, I'll start with disgruntled muttering.

And you know, you gotta consider the source. Dylan Thomas never made it to the Big Four-O. At thirty-something, I could have raged with the best of them. But at thirty-something, I can't imagine what a person would have to rage against.

On the other hand, being subjected to prolonged

bouts of TV has taught me that there may be other ways to increase my energy level. It seems that Vitayumkins for Seniors will restore my youthful vigor. And I can get a second mega-bottle free, if I order right now.

THE LAST TIME I SAW GEORGE

Golden Hills is the name of the place. Talk about misnomers. But then, that's what we do, isn't it? Everything's got spin.

Going through the double glass doors that open into the foyer, the first-time visitor would not be unimpressed. The carpet looks new. The parlor-like setting, with its overstuffed chairs adjacent to pseudo-Victorian tables, conveys an almost comfortable impression. The light is neither blinding nor dim; an eye-soothing medium wattage illuminates the pale beige walls. In the corners, live plants thrive. At center stage stands a large fish tank with dappled denizens dangling languidly. Somewhere in the background, a melody by a stringed ensemble drifts soothingly. But something is out of place.

That something is the smell of stale urine and decaying flesh that the scented candles don't quite cover. Inquiring relatives might never identify this incongruity, for it is in this room that the business of admissions is conducted. Only by specific demand will the family of the potential resident become acquainted with the wards spoking out gulag-fashion from the formal greeting area. At least this is true initially. Later, learning the unpleasant truth is unavoidable.

For sure, though, there's nothing the color of gold. And if there are any hills around, they're neatly camouflaged as flat city streets within a failing neighborhood. Golden Hills is a nursing home at which I am not, thank God, a resident.

Why I'm here is because of my Uncle George. And since Uncle George mostly raised me, I make the pilgrimage out to this place every couple of days to visit.

Now there's a chuckle – "visit" I mean. A visit is when you go see someone and you talk about things of mutual interest. Our usual drill is not quite that.

"Hi, Uncle George," I always say when I walk into his room.

Most times, Uncle George is sleeping. If he's not, I get the glare that says "Who in the hell are you?" Or maybe just a vacant stare as he drools.

"How's it goin'?" I always ask.

How's it going? Right! George doesn't have a clue. Sometimes I just sit there and read. Sometimes I read out loud to George if his latest roommate has, shall we say, moved on. Occasionally I just talk off the top of my head, saying outrageous things to see if I can get some reaction.

Nothing.

It's not that I'm every uncle's dream nephew. But what nephew would go visit an uncle in Golden Hills more than one time? When my folks were killed in a car crash many years ago, ol' George was the only thing between me and a government-run child protective service. He raised me like a son. Although I call him "Uncle," it could just as easily be "Dad."

I'm not casting aspersions at all nephews universally. Really, though, you'd have to have a very unusual relationship with your father's brother to want to experience Golden Hills ever, but certainly no more than once.

Golden Hills is a netherworld between life and death. The people, and I use that word loosely, are not going to recover. This is the waiting area to get on the train to whatever's down the tracks.

Apparently the people running Golden Hills believe that all its residents are going to hell, or nowhere at all, after they die. I say this because if the friendly staff believed that the residents might have some power in the afterlife, they'd treat them a lot better. And maybe they're right. Most assuredly, fat Helen – ostensibly deaf to residents' pleas for just about anything – would by now have been haunted to insanity by departed former residents if that were possible. I mean, I've seen butchers more caring and sensitive to slabs of beef.

So if it's such a hellhole, why is George here? Money. He didn't have any. I don't have any. And without it, Golden Hills is the best we can do.

"But why don't *you* take care of him?" you ask.

The easy answer is I gotta work at least eight hours a day. So I can't be there to take care of George. And, yeah, you're right. I don't want to. George is no longer six feet tall and two hundred pounds, but he's still a grown man – kinda. More like a very large, totally helpless infant. I can't handle that – physically or emotionally. So here we are in Golden Hills.

*****

"Hi, Helen!" I say this cheerfully, as usual, as I pass the nurses' station, walking again through the ward to nowhere.

I know that Helen may or may not look up from whatever she is continually doing behind the counter. In any case, the best I can expect is a grunt. But I do not wish to in any way anger Helen. She is bad enough undisturbed. Who knows what she might do if motivated?

As I move in the direction of Uncle George's room, a wheelchair angles to cut me off. Naturally, the chair is not entirely empty. Its guiding force is a person of indecipherable sex whose single unshod foot scuffs the linoleum tile to provide forward motion.

"Hey, how ya doin'?" I chirp, neatly dodging a collision.

The foot that moves the chair stops. The creature in control says nothing, merely looks into my eyes. And the look tells the tale. It is one of unfocused anger – a probing glance straining mightily, but failing, to comprehend the rationality of the situation before it, and demanding an account for this circumstance.

What can I say? This is not foreign to me. I move

around the wheelchair and continue my mission.

Somewhere to my left, from the shroud of sheets that is a bedroom, comes the sound of moans. Perhaps it is pain. More likely, I think, it is despair.

I can quicken my pace to avoid the moaner, but the odor is inescapable. It is the odor of poorly kept convalescent places everywhere. To me, it will always be the odor of lurking lingering death.

At last I reach the relative comfort of Uncle George's room. The milieu is no better, but at least it's more familiar. No stranger will accost me. The constant noise of the wall-mounted TV blocks the omnipresent sound of anguish.

"How's it goin', Uncle George?"

I don't expect a response and don't get one. Today I have no book. So I babble.

"Hey, how 'bout them dawgs?" Neither George, nor I, nor anyone I know attended the University of Georgia, but for some reason I know there has been a football game and the topic provides fodder. "I mean to tell ya. Kicked Florida's butt. Score's thirty-six to seven. I mean there's no joy in Gainesville tonight." That monologue plays out.

"Whadaya think about the big fight?" Pause for no

particular reason. "Tyson? Naw. Winnie the Pooh and Tigger. Tigger's favored. Younger. Better shape. Longer teeth and claws. But that Pooh can take a punch."

To appreciate the doggerel, if in fact that's possible, you've got to understand that almost everything has no meaning for Uncle George. He's been with no awareness of the world around him for some time, even the world inside Golden Hills. He knows nothing of 9/11, of Iraq's machinations, of the Super Bowl or the World Series, or anything else I might mention.

"Did ya hear the Pope ran off with Mother Teresa?" George was a devout Catholic. No reaction. Just the vacant stare of incomprehension.

The adrenaline – or caffeine or whatever – seems to be dissipating from my body. The doughty flippancy I have maintained fades. I probe the depths of Uncle George's stare with my own as I recall the good times of our life together.

"You're not in there, are you, Uncle George?" I am almost moved to tears by his inability to understand. "I know you don't understand, but I love you." I lean close and whisper, like maybe the guy in the next bed could understand the meaning of my words. I pause and take my uncle's hand.

"Got to go. See you in a couple of days." I place his hand on the sheet and turn to leave.

"Eh!" A husky breathy noise comes from the direction of George.

I turn, wondering if someone left the call-system microphone in his bedding. The first thing I notice is that George's eyes are no longer empty. Somehow the spark of life has been reignited there. It's now my turn to stare.

"Uncle George?!"

The faintest hint of a smile plays across his lips.

"Can you understand me?"

Slowly, very slowly, George surveys me and his immediate environment. Then he grimaces.

"Where?" he huffs with great effort.

"Uncle George, you're in a nursing home. You've been here a long time."

"Oh, yeah. You doin' OK?" The words dribble from his lips as if individually formed and expelled. I must lean close to hear.

"Hey, I'm fine. You're the one we're worried about." Absurdly – maybe I got that from TV – I use the first person plural. There is no "we" – only me.

George manages what might loosely be called a grin.

"Can I get you something? Water?" Why is it that we always think a little food or water is bound to help whatever might be wrong?

George moves his head in weak negation.

"How're you doin'?" I am astounded that my uncle is back. What do you say to a person who has suddenly appeared from who-knows-where?

"OK. Only…"

I now have my ear next to his mouth. "Only?" I'm not sure I've got it right.

"… not here." His words are so gradual and soft, it could almost be a faint summer breeze.

"You mean you're OK but you can't tell me here? You mean…" I have no idea what he means. "You mean you think you're somewhere else?"

Uncle George averts his eyes in a gesture with which I'm very familiar. He thinks I'm clearly a moron and he's doing me the courtesy of stifling a laugh.

"Well, what!!!? Uncle George, I don't understand 'OK, only not here'."

Again, the hint of a smile and a nod. "Love you." His

voice is now almost completely indecipherable, tailing off to nothing.

"I love you, too, Uncle George."

I take his timeworn and needle-ravaged hand. My lips are tightly pursed as I once more search his eyes with mine. But the spark has vanished.

After a while, getting no further response to my own voice, I take my leave. Perhaps my confusion moves me. I approach fat Helen as I wander past the nurses' station.

"Is George gettin' better?" I demand.

"Huh?" Helen looks up.

"George, in room 202. He recognized me. He just spoke to me."

"Naw, probably not. They all do that now and then. It's too bad."

Could this be a flash of humanity in Helen?

"Yeah." I slump. "They're so out of it."

"That's not it. The reverse." Helen is almost indignant. "It's them scintillas, you know. That's their problem."

"Yeah." I make the nod of understanding. Then I pause. "No! I don't know. Whadaya mean?"

"Them last bright flickers of knowin' stuff before

they go back for good." Helen's tone is almost dreamy.

Now I'm looking at Helen like maybe she's been into the sample meds. "Back from where?"

"I don't know." She shrugs. "But that's where most of 'em stay."

My look in response to this revelation apparently irritates Helen.

"You really think anyone could live in this place for long?" Helen challenges.

Now it's my turn to shrug.

"Humph," she puffs. "Go look in their eyes. All look just like George. They're not here."

At this point my mouth opens. I want to say something, but I don't know what.

"Call it what you want." Helen pauses to watch me before she continues. "Body's reaction to stress, maybe. I say it's a gift from God. He lets 'em go to limbo or whatever 'til their body finishes up with its business here. Man's not meant to live this long, but man don't know that. He thinks he's supposed to live forever. So we keep pumpin' 'em full of stuff. And see what happens? But God knows. And even though man's messin' where he shouldn't, He cuts 'em some slack."

"Eh," I say, give an idiot grin, and walk out.

As I drive home, I wonder about Helen. In fact, my thoughts return to Helen often.

I hope she's right.

REDUX

Call me Mick – not because I'm akin to the rock'n'roll star of the same name, but because I've just finished being a mouse.

If you're thinking: *What's that all about?* let me explain.

You see, I've been many things in many past lives. Last time, it was rodent city for me. If you're interested, this is how it works. You start out somewhere, depending on the Big Man's whim, and try to work up from there. So you might, for instance, start out as a ground slug. If you're a really good ground slug, next time you might come back as a dog – maybe. If you're a really good dog, Lassie class, you might come back as a chimpanzee. And so on and so on.

However, there's a catch. There's always a catch. In

the military, it's up or out. In the game of life, it's up or down. So let's say you've made it to dog, but instead of being brave and saving people all the time, you spend your time chasing cars or biting the mailman on the butt. The next time around, it's back down the evolutionary ladder. Perhaps a mouse.

But that's not how I got here. My "progress" is kinda like a triple backwards jump. I had finally made the A-team on the last go-round. The big show. *Homo sapiens.* Unfortunately – God knows why (which happens to be the truth) – I chose a very tricky career path. I was a politician. Even made it to Congress. If I had been a dog, that would be like raising the old leg on an altar… and then biting the priest on the butt on the way out. So last time, it was all the way back to mouse.

"That's silly," you say. "If you know the consequences of your behavior, why would you choose to be a bad dog or a politician?"

I don't want to get off into philosophy – free will and all that – but here's a clue: the game is not rigged in your favor. More to the point, the only time you know about the game is before and after. If I were still a mouse or a politician, I wouldn't know about the rules of the game. While you're whatever you are in whatever world you're in, your only ink-ling of what you had been or what you might become is an occasional *déjà vu* experience, or some holy guy telling you to behave and give him money or you'll end up a ground slug or some such.

"Hmm," you say, "and why are you telling me this?"

Well, mostly because I can. In fact, it's the only time I can. Maybe you'll take this to heart and not end up as a mouse yourself. Maybe because my life as a mouse was a bit unusual and I don't want you to be put off by the story of a sometimes-talking, reasoning mouse. We do mazes pretty well, but that's about it.

You see, when you've been around a long time – many recycles – sometimes you come back with some pretty unusual gifts. Maybe sometimes The Maestro gets bored with the game. How fun could it be watching His subjects contin-ually go back to square one? So to advance things, He gives you some extra talent to help you out. How otherwise would you account for a Lance Armstrong, an Albert Einstein, or a Mother Teresa?

Of course, to whom much is given, much is expected. There's a serious downside to doing poorly even with the extra help. I won't talk about that except to say it's a hell of a deal. So pay attention.

When my eyes first opened, I was scrunched into a nest that I would later learn sat in a big field next to a large house. Of course, it wasn't just me. I had two brothers and three sisters and Mom. Very tight quarters. Mom apparently hadn't planned on quite so many of us. Either that, or mother mouses only know how to build limited kinds of mouse houses. Dad was nowhere around. I don't hold that against him. That's what father mouses do: show up for the sex and then bolt.

Like I said, my name was Mick. There was also Marko, Milton, Minnie, Mabel, and Ditz. Ditz was the last one born, and I don't think she came through with her share of the gene pool. Hence the name. Actually, Mom didn't name anybody. Mouses don't really have names. Those names were given by me so I could keep up with all these new mouses. Baby mouses are very hard to tell apart.

At first, life wasn't bad. Most of the time we slept. Usually, early in the morning, Mom would wake us, roll over on her side, and we took it from there.

Early on, I learned that mouses don't talk – at least, not like human beings. One morning after breakfast, I complained, "Mom, I'm still hungry." That caused Mom to jump up and run out of the nest, and we didn't see her for a couple of days. About the only thing a mouse is supposed to say is "squeak." For a mouse, speech in any human language is like the go-button for the survival response. From then on, I confined myself to "squeak" or sometimes, depending on the urgency of my need, "squeak, squeak, squeak."

After a while, Mom refused to roll over on her side to let us feed. What she did instead was push us out of the nest and demonstrate how to eat grass, plants, and nuts. Personally, I liked the milk better, but that was a done deal.

It was during the first or second eating demonstration out of the nest that Ditz disappeared. The rest of us stayed close to Mom trying to learn what would and what would not cause us not to feel hungry. For me, it was a no-brainer: growing things, or things that had been growing, were good to eat; live things, like other mouses, and dead things, like dirt, didn't do the job. Milton didn't seem to get it, and as time went on, he began to look funny. Marko, Minnie, and Mabel caught on pretty quickly.

We never did find out what happened to Ditz. One minute she was there; the next she wasn't. Oddly enough, I was the only one who seemed to care.

In fact, no one but me seemed to care when Milton began to lose weight and look even grayer than he was to begin with. So, being a good brother, every time he tried to eat something like dirt, I nipped him on the tail. In fairly short order, he seemed to grasp that if he ate some things, he felt better and didn't get nipped on the tail. Unfortunately, I didn't have time to follow Milton around all the time. So Milton's diet pretty much consisted of green grass and an occasional nut. But that was the best I could do, and Milton seemed to be happy with it.

Fairly quickly – it had to be pretty quick; mouses don't live very long – we developed into grown-up mouses. Milton, Marko, Minnie, and Mabel began to treat Mom like just another mouse. My reward for showing deference was that Mom ate my food, and she'd nip me when I tried to nurse. It was when Minnie and Marko seemed to have "a thing" going that I realized mouses don't have much of an attention span.

If that's the way it was, so be it. Besides that, by then

I was bigger, stronger, quicker, and, if I do say so myself, better looking than anyone in my family. At least Mabel seemed to think so. I no longer needed Mom or any of them. However, I must admit that Mabel began to look better and better. Something about the way she swished her tail, I think.

Although we still remained a family – very loosely defined – we kind of paired off: me and Mabel, Marko and Minnie, and Milton and Mom. Mouses don't seem to care about the Oedipal thing.

Rapidly I learned everything that Mom could teach. Because I was actually a superior mouse as well, I became the leader, and things would have been just fine for the rest of our mousey lives. I could control the other mouses to the extent that they shared their food with me, and occasionally Minnie, Mabel, and Mom all spent "quality time" with me.

But – there's always a but – Marko wasn't happy with the situation. If you ranked us by any criterion, Marko would have been a way-distant second, but that was close enough for Marko to actually believe that he just might be the superior mouse. He began to refuse to share his food with me, and once, when Minnie came to visit me, Marko bit me... hard on the tail.

Well, after Marko figured out how to remove his tail from one particular orifice, he never directly confronted me again. It seems that mouses retain some lessons better than others. However, he became deliberately disruptive to my kingdom and demonstrated passive-aggressive behavior at every opportunity.

When Mom, Mabel, Minnie, and I were together, Marko would squeak loudly and in an odd tempo. It was a lot like a faucet dripping in the middle of the night – impossible to concentrate.

When I gave that certain whisker-swish that signaled it was time to forage, Marko would lift one foot and limp around as if he were in pain. Minnie, of course, and some-times Mom and Mabel would go to investigate. Naturally that caused a delay in my foraging schedule.

Worst of all, Marko would attempt to take the lead when we finally did manage to start the forage. In the latter case, it was necessary for me to demonstrate that I was, in fact, the superior mouse. Then he'd roll around like he was really hurt, and the girls – and sometimes Milton, who seemed to be a little gender-confused – would have to inves-tigate, which meant more delay.

However, even with Marko's antics, I was recognized as the boss. I like to think it was my sleek brown fur and beautiful beady brown eyes that promoted the loyalty – at least with the girls. But there were other things, like the time when we had been tempted into the open by the discovery of a large pile of nuts left unattended by whoever had gathered them. While the others dashed for the free grub, I surveyed the area, noting no apparent danger and a fairly accessible escape-hole. Then, when the shadow of wings engulfed us, I gave the "triple-squeak tail-wag red alert" signal just in time to avoid the talons of some winged predatory monster. Boy, that got their attention. It was nuts and romance for a week. Then they seemed to forget why they were treating me so special and quit.

I did suggest that it might be better if we hung around the nest during the daytime, and did most of our foraging at night. If you've ever tried to convey a concept to a mouse, you know how difficult this was. I did the only thing I could think of, refusing to give my forage signal during the day and nipping tails if someone else did. It seemed to work.

You couldn't say these were troubled times. Mouses, even Marko, aren't very difficult to intimidate. So my life was pretty good for a mouse. Little did I know that this was just the calm before the storm. Marko had not given up on his quest to become the alpha mouse.

During one of our nightly forages through the neighboring field, I noticed the absence of Marko. *It'd sure be a tough break if he had met up with our friend, the garden snake*, I thought. But that was not the case.

Later, around first light, who showed up but Marko. *Great.* The surprising thing was that he was carrying something big and yellow and wonderful-smelling in his two little front teeth. This was something new to all of us.

Proudly he strutted around the nest swishing his tail. After a loud squeak from me, he dropped his prize and allowed us to check it out. Sniffing proved almost orgasmic and the taste was beyond comprehension. If mouses could put together a belief system centered around deity, we would all have become converts right then. But mouses can't even remember not to mate with their mothers, so that didn't happen. What did happen was we all followed Marko, me reluctantly, when it was time to forage the next night.

Instead of taking our normal protected route out to the field, Marko turned toward the large house. *Good going,*

Marko, I thought sarcastically. *You're gonna run into a wall in about three more yards*. But he didn't. Right at the foot of the large stone wall was a hole. Marko went in. We followed.

I want to say for the record that I didn't think this was such a good idea. Mom had never taken us here before and we'd all seen strange things near that wall – humans, dogs, cats even. All I could think of to do was warn against this adventure. And the only way I could do it quickly was to use my human voice. Unfortunately, when I tried, I had forgotten how. It had been too long. I followed.

Up and around and down between and under things we went. Marko seemed to know where he was going. At last, we came to a large area with not much for cover. Near a wall in a corner sat a huge piece of the yellow ambrosia.

Like starved sharks in a feeding frenzy, my family darted to the yellow paradise. Even I, usually cautious and circumspect, was sucked into the frenzy. However, I fought the pull and, as a result, Marko was first to the prize. With great bravado, he snatched the yellow delight and magnanimously shared it with the rest of us. *The mark of a leader?* I mused. *I think not.*

Even a large piece of food wasn't enough for six hungry mouses. Marko lead on. I, however, hesitated long enough to study the scene of the first feast. The yellow stuff had apparently been placed on some contraption. Being a very intelligent and mechanically-minded mouse, I perceived that where the food had been was a murderous device for the purpose of killing mouses. One false move would cause the thing to slam shut in just about the area where a mouse's head might be.

In the distance, about ten feet, I could see my family approaching yet another murder device holding an even bigger parcel of the fabulous food. Of course, it was Marko who moved directly toward the goal. He had been successful at least twice, but I didn't know if he could do it again. Marko didn't know one way or the other, or anything at all for that matter. He was just snatching free food and dazzling the dollies.

I decided that, because of my super-mousely speed and agility, I could make it to the trap before Marko had a chance to bring death raining down on his head (literally). But then I stopped. *What are you doin', Mick? This is your chance to be rid of that goof forever. Ease off. Let nature take its course. You'll be back in charge with no pretenders and no one will be blamed except that idiot, Marko.*

Then another thought struck me: *What if he does it again? They really will think he's the new leader. Can't let that happen.*

Engaging my extra powerful mousey muscles, in the blink of an eye I was at the trap just as Marko made his matador move to snag the prize. Pushing Marko to safety with one paw, my momentum carried me right into the jaws of death. *Ouch.*

From above, or beyond, or wherever, I witnessed the momentary shock and surprise on the faces of my family. Then I watched them all eating the cheese over my dead body.

"Mouses are such a fickle lot," I cried in disgust.

And that's it.

"What's it?" you ask. "What happened with your coming back? Is it up or down?"

"Well… Hold on a second. It's the red phone." A minute or two passes as I listen. "The Word is I've gone far enough. Seems there's a line here that mortals, even between cycles, don't get to cross. But you're a smart guy. You can figure it out. Sorry. Gotta go. It's time to start my life as a…."

SIC SEMPER BUTCH GRAMMER

It was autumn and I felt like autumn.

On the one hand, it was a brilliant sunny day – "crisp" is the descriptor. The wind blew sporadically, causing brilliant reds and golds to swirl and flutter lifelessly to the sidewalk. Those were the early quitters. Above and all around were the stalwarts clinging hardily to the ancient boughs, creating an almost miraculous tunnel of fall splendor backlit by south-advancing sun. Somewhere beyond sight but not imagination, twenty-two men fought valiantly for the glory of their *alma mater* as their fellows cheered them on. The effect was invigorating – even warming with the cords and woolen sweater.

On the other hand, just beyond the dazzle of the season lay the metaphor. It was the closing of things. Nature's last hurrah before what had been verdant and vigorous descended into that final pale of cold and dead. And as the song says, the days do "get shorter when you reach September."

It was that second meaning of autumn that was bothersome, but I resolved to shake it off and experience the moment – *perhaps the last such moment* echoed my resolve.

"Phooey." I reacted aloud to the echo. "You're only sixty-seven. Get a grip, dude."

Several of the park's other naturephiles reacted to this old man speaking to no one. I ducked my cap and moved away, sucking in the spectacular day. I would not be troubled by dark specters.

It was City Park on a Saturday. Dogs and children played on the lawn. Near the center of the park was an area with benches surrounding a pond. This center was where the old men sat with their memories. *And young lovers launching on the journey into life's greatest and most peculiar pleasure*, I mentally corrected. Clearly this was also a time for new beginnings.

In fact, I was beginning to feel the stir of life as my line of sight settled on one striking young woman. Voyeuristic guilt, I suppose, caused me to shift my eyes to one of the bench duffers. However, all things considered, it could have been fate. For sitting there in a black overcoat staring at nothing in particular was a familiar face from school, years and years ago.

And, like everything on this day, the memories were mixed.

I had known Butch… eh, something. *Ah, the wonder of aging*, I digressed. But no matter. I had known Butch Whoever from first grade to high-school graduation. Then lost track of him. Rumor had it that he was killed in the war. It was good to see this part of my past alive.

The other part of the memory was of Butch Grammer – the name returned from somewhere in my aging neuronal tangle – the big red-faced bully who seemed to thrive on tormenting those of smaller stature, and me in particular.

It must have been first or second grade when I first became painfully aware of Butchie, as he was known then. I had filed in from the playground to my seat near the back of the classroom. Our teacher had ranked us in order of behavior: the troublemakers sat up front where the teacher could get to them easily.

"That's my seat, budroe." Butchie – big (to me, at least), red-faced, and threatening.

"No," I replied with confidence. "Mrs. Taylor told me to sit here."

"You see this?" Butchie, even redder in the face, held up a mammoth left fist. "I'm gonna knock your teeth down your throat if you don't get outta my seat."

Since I had just lost a tooth the week before, when it fell out for no apparent reason, I was convinced that Butchie could make good on his promise. Heck, even if I had all my permanent teeth, he could probably make good on his promise.

As I was weighing the merits of losing all my teeth or disobeying Mrs. Taylor, salvation came in the form of Mrs. Taylor.

"Butchie Grammer, you get right up here where I told you to sit." This wasn't an idle statement. Mrs. Taylor had Butchie firmly grasped by his ear and was dragging him to his assigned seat. Butchie did not cry. He just turned redder in the face, giving me a ferocious look.

Hey, it wasn't my fault, I foolishly reasoned. But Butchie apparently thought it was and that was enough for Butchie. In my heart of hearts, I knew that this was the start of something terrible.

It was maybe the next day toward the end of an arithmetic lesson. I was focusing all my young power of concentration on the solution to seven-minus-four when I happened to glance down the row of desks. There, crawling on all fours, was Butchie.

In no time, he had grabbed my left arm, twisting it vigorously. "Now, teacher's pet, I'm gonna break your arm off and beat you to death with it," he hissed.

What's a boy to do? I thought as I screamed, turning in the direction of my tormentor, hoping to push him away. Unfortunately for Butchie, I had forgotten to put down my pencil. So the push was more of a stab right into Butchie's forehead. That caused Butchie to let go – and scream as well.

The "why" of Butchie's being at my desk apparently escaped Mrs. Taylor. What she saw was Butchie screaming with my pencil stuck in his bloody forehead.

Well, the result was not all bad. I was, of course, moved to the front of the classroom. There were calls back and forth between our respective parents. Even with my explanation, I was subjected to a session with "the belt." How-ever, everyone concerned, at least every adult concerned, made it clear that Butchie and I were not to even think about getting close to each other… anywhere… ever.

I was completely happy with the result. Butchie was not and vowed vengeance. Of course, I was safe as long as I was in school or at home in my neighborhood. But Butchie managed to corner me on the way home from school a few weeks later. After a verbal thrashing and a few punches, I guess Butchie thought we were even. After that, I stayed as far away from Butchie in grade school as possible and never mentioned his revenge. Baleful stares and occasional taunts were the extent of our interaction – until we reached junior high school.

Really though, in junior high, Butch, as he was now called, and I did alright. In those days, several grade schools fed into a junior high school. That meant lots of new kids. For Butch, that meant lots of new kids to pick on. He really didn't have a lot of time to devote to me.

One of the new kids was Skip Terrell. Skip was big, captain of the wrestling team, and my new best friend. Only once did Butch bother me in junior high, and after a "conversation" with Skip, that happened no more.

That's not to say that I lost track of Butch in junior high. He was one of those kids who was always making trouble – usually for someone else. Although he couldn't be totally avoided, Skip or no Skip, I made sure I knew where Butch was and tried my best not to be there.

My final encounter with Butch Grammer came during my sophomore year in high school. Butch had gotten much bigger and much meaner. I had grown as well, but unfortunately not as much or as fast as Butch. And the final event, so to speak, didn't involve flying fists or bloodshed. It was much worse.

I was coming out of the gym locker room, hurrying to English class. As always, the halls were crowded with young men and women trying hard to be cool and sophisticated – in a high-school kind of way. Suddenly, from behind, strong hands grabbed me and held me in place while other hands removed my pants… both sets. Then I was pushed to the floor. Looking up, half naked, I stared into the big red face of good ol' Butch.

"You want these, geek-o?" Butch paused menacingly, twirling my pants in the air. "Well, you can take 'em, if you think you're big enough. Or, if you're just your basic little chickenshit, I'll leave 'em for you… on the flagpole."

What followed was the longest two or three minutes in my life. There I was on the floor naked with all the kids, even the girls, staring at me. Not that I was all that hot to get in a fight with Butch Grammer in any condition, but naked? In front of the student body? Not likely. I bolted for the locker room.

At some point toward the end of the school day, the assistant principal found me in the locker room, hidden in the linen closet. Always helpful, he handed me my pants as he made a half-hearted attempt to indict me for hanging them on the flagpole. Then he let that slide, telling me I had to report to detention hall for missing a day's worth of classes.

From that day forward, my high-school experience was a disaster. For three years, I was known as "the naked guy" by my fellow students. Once I heard one teacher telling another that he had the naked guy in his class. None of the boys, even my ex-friend Skip Terrell, wanted to have the naked guy for a buddy, and dating the naked guy was kind of like a statement of non-virtue for the girls.

But high school ended… finally. With time, and a college far far away, bitter memory faded. I don't know if Butch ever graduated, but I heard he was drafted. As far as I knew, or cared, that was it for Butch and me.

At least that was it until now.

Memories I had thought long relegated to restless nights came flooding back. The image of the big ugly red-faced bully standing over me taunting me with my pants overwhelmed me. The flashback of girls tittering in the halls as I scurried to classes made my stomach tighten. The angry ruminations of "what if" I'd done this or that rang in my ears. Now here that son-of-a-bitch was. And he was no longer big and I was no longer frightened.

Striding to the bench where Butch sat, I confronted him, heedless of onlookers.

"Butch Grammer?" I demanded.

"You got it, pardner. Who wants to know?" he sneered.

Releasing the years of pent-up anger, I bitch-slapped Butch hard enough to rock his head back and almost unseat him. "On your knees, asshole. Make me believe you're sorry before I grind your ass into the dirt."

Sounded good, but that was just a quick fantasy that

bounced through my head as I moved slowly, but deliberately, in his direction. I'm not saying it might not have happened as fantasized, but as I neared Butch, I noticed that his black overcoat was tattered around the edges and smudged with dirt. The fiery red hair had degenerated to tufts of white protruding from beneath a wrinkled gray dress hat. He still had the scarlet complexion, but that was mostly due to a series of broken veins interlaced with patches of white beard. If Albert Einstein had been an unwashed, emaciated street person, he would have cast the same aura as the Butch I now closely faced. Even at my age, a fist fight would have been no contest.

Wherever his mind had been, it suddenly refocused on me. Blinking for a moment, he said, "Got a dollar for a guy down on his luck?"

Now unsure of my own perception, I asked, "Butch Grammer?"

Seeming unsure, he paused, then nodded. "Yeah, Butch Grammer. That's me."

We stared at each other across the years. I bridged the gap. He apparently didn't. "Do I know you from somewhere?" he asked.

"Yeah, I think so. J.J. Preston, R.T. Mathers, and Bryan Adams," I said, trying to jog his memory.

"Oh," was all he said, canting his head as his eyes lost focus again. "Yeah," he mused. "Those were the schools I went to."

Then his eyes sharpened on my face as if it were all coming back to him. "You were a teacher, weren't you?"

"No," I answered tentatively. "We were in the same class."

Butch idly stroked his beard, thinking. "Yeah. There were lots of kids in my class." He eyed me again, almost suspiciously. "Are you a cop now?"

"No, Butch. I teach computer science at the college." I nodded off in the direction of the university. "I was just walking when I saw you, and thought I'd say 'Hi.' It's been a long time."

"Yeah, I guess it has. Lotta water, you know."

"What happened to you after high school? Somebody said you died in the war."

"No. Didn't die. Don't know for sure. Something happened. Something bad. Been in and out of lots of VA hospitals. Don't even know how many. Kinda lost count."

He seemed to be trying to figure out how many hospitals.

"You don't remember me, do you?" I gave him my name.

I could almost see the wheels turning as he tried, but failed, to place me. "Guess not. I'm sure we were pals. You seem like a nice guy."

It was all I could do to keep the tears back. All these years I had hated this rat-bastard, but even Butch Grammer, my nemesis, didn't deserve to end up like this.

"I've done pretty well, Butch. Let me give you some money," I mumbled as I slid a hundred-dollar bill into his withered hand. "Buy something you need."

His eyes widened as he noted the denomination of the bill. His eyes looked wet.

That seemed to be the end of the conversation.

"Gotta go," I said by way of an exit line. "Take care of yourself." I turned and walked away.

From over my shoulder, I heard him call out. "Maybe when I get back on my feet, I'll buy you a new pair of pants. Yar har har har."

I turned just in time to see him disappearing behind the hedge toward the park exit.

TIME TO KILL

In seventy years of life, Roger Gordon had never seen the inside of a police station – except, of course, on TV. And this one wasn't at all like Barney Miller's place somewhere in New York or Fort Apache in the Bronx. This was more like a hospital with a nurse's desk and long halls spoking out to various offices. There didn't seem to be a "lock up" or a "bull-pen" where criminals were kept or cops worked at their desks.

Actually, when he was arrested – if that was truly what had happened – it was more like an invitation to a meeting or something. He wasn't handcuffed. The cops seemed like nice guys – friendly, polite. He wondered how exactly Rodney King had gotten in that mess. Roger was a black man, too. So it wasn't a race thing.

When they arrived at the police station, the cops had asked that he have a seat on a bench along one of the long hallways. They said it would be a minute before they could talk. *Apparently*, Roger thought, *these guys have a little problem with time*. It had now been almost an hour and he was getting tired, or bored, or both.

His mind wandered to what was probably the beginning of this whole sorry affair. It was at a self-defense seminar for seniors. The speaker was some kind of martial arts expert.

*****

"Look," the speaker began. "What all this comes down to is how bad do you want to live?"

When the speaker was introduced to the group – a bunch of older men and women – it was clear that the guy could probably crack steel with his tongue. Black belt in this and that. Special Forces in several wars. Covert ops in one "hot spot" and another. Ramrod straight with the look of a coiled spring, albeit an old spring. Roger wondered if he could just take this guy home with him and not worry about the rest of the stuff.

"These dirtball criminals are not nice guys. They're not gonna give you a break because you're a senior citizen. The reason they've picked you is *because* you're a senior citizen who they believe will not be able to defend himself or herself. And that is the only advantage you have."

Everyone was listening closely.

"What I mean is that these lurkers think you're defenseless, and that may make them careless. Normally there'll be one or two of them. One is more dangerous. He's planned it out and he's gonna get right to business. Not always, but when there's two, they'll be playing off each other to get their courage up. That may give you your chance. If you're not lucky, the first thing you know about an attack is when you see stars. Or you may never know because you're dead."

That little factoid caused a definite ripple in the crowd.

"But we're gonna assume you're not dead. Wham, they hit you and say 'Gimme your money.' If they have masks on, do it. If you see their faces, the chances get better that they won't want to leave any witnesses. In that second case, you gotta decide whether you want to just die or go down fighting. And you never know. You might win or at least take enough time for a lucky break to happen."

The speaker had much to say about the many ways a weaker person could potentially carry the day in a confrontation with stronger criminals. Roger didn't think he'd ever be able to physically defeat a younger stronger man. Maybe ten or fifteen years ago, but now he was just too weak to fight and too slow to run. In his younger days Roger had been quite a scrapper, and he had held on to that image until it became clear, even to Roger, that he wasn't even close to being the man he used to be. However, the seminar had given Roger a few valuable pieces of information.

"First, pay attention to what's going on around you. Walk away from a bad situation. If you feel something bad's gonna happen, it probably is. Never allow yourself to be caught off guard. Second, take the initiative. Don't wait for it to happen to you. TV always portrays good guys as waiting for the bad guy to make the first move. TV is a fantasyland. You snooze, you lose. If it looks like something's comin' down and you can't get away, move first. Third, buy a gun, learn how to shoot it, and keep it handy. You may not get a chance to use it, but wouldn't it be a bitch if you had a chance to save your life, but you didn't have anything to save it with?

Don't be concerned with the attacker taking your gun away and using it against you. The dirtbag was gonna use something against you anyway. Whether it turns out to be your gun, his gun, a knife, a club, or he just beats you to death with his fists doesn't really matter much."

*****

Officer... Roger couldn't remember his last name, but his first name was Mike. Officer Mike came out of somewhere after a while, and said he was sorry for the delay. He said there had been some kind of big explosion downtown, and cops were being called in from everywhere in the city on a priority basis. There was some suspicion of a terrorist attack. Officer Mike thought this was silly. "What right thinkin' terrorist would attack downtown? Hell, it's been vacant for years. But that's our government in action."

Officer Mike said he was sorry that Roger couldn't leave, but he said he'd get to Roger just as soon as he could. In the meantime, he told Roger where the coffee shop was and showed him a phone he could use to call his wife.

Roger thought coffee was going to be necessary if he was going to stay awake. It was long past Roger's bedtime and it had been some kind of a day.

The coffee tasted pretty terrible, but it was strong, and in no time at all Roger was sitting on the same bench, bored but awake.

*****

Roger had gone to his local gun shop and explained to the helpful clerk that he needed a weapon for protection. The helpful clerk suggested an assault rifle or a modified shotgun. Roger had chuckled at that and said that all he wanted was some kind of small handgun.

The helpful clerk seemed unhappy about Roger's preference. Roger reckoned that handguns were less expensive than rifles or shotguns.

"You know, mister," the helpful clerk said, "if you shoot someone with a little pistol, it might just piss 'em off. And the bluff value of a little gun's not much. Besides, you don't ever want to pull a gun on someone if you're not gonna use it."

Roger wondered if that last bit of advice was valid, but he let it go and asked the helpful clerk what he would recommend.

The helpful clerk began with .44s and .45s, moved to .357s, and finally, reluctantly, showed Roger a .38 snub-nosed revolver. This was more of what Roger had had in mind, but it was still too big.

"What about that one?" he inquired.

The helpful clerk turned up his nose. "Well, with a dum-dum, you'd have the knockdown power. I guess it'd work. But you'd have to learn to shoot it." The helpful clerk, at Roger's request, explained that a "dum-dum" was a bullet blunted at the business end. That way, when it hit a target, it would spread out and do more damage.

Roger was happy because it looked like a nice little gun and wasn't all that expensive. The helpful clerk was happy because, although the gun Roger selected wasn't as expensive as the others, the lessons he would give Roger would balance it out.

Roger had learned to shoot. He'd never be a marksman, but he could put five bullets – that's all his little gun would hold – in a man-shaped target at twenty yards. Not bad for a guy who'd never held a gun before.

Roger decided that he would not seek a permit to carry his gun. He didn't want to carry it into public places like the grocery store or his doctor's office, and he didn't really go out that much anyway. He would keep it in his car when he did go out; otherwise it would stay in his home. He dismissed the issue of legality. Why would anyone want to arrest a seventy-year-old man for carrying a gun in his car?

It was sometime after the purchase of the gun and the lessons when Roger was reading the morning paper with his wife. It seemed that the newest criminal venture was called "home invasion." Although it sounded like something the government might do, it was actually a combination of burglary and robbery. Instead of attacking somewhere in public, the robbers would gain entrance to a home, bind or kill the residents, and take what valuables they could find.

For Roger, the intrusive nature of the act into a hitherto sacrosanct place made it a truly scary crime. Plus, the idea of some worthless piece of garbage taking hard-earned valuables from Roger – perhaps Roger's life, his wife's life – made him angry and determined not to let it happen without a fight. Roger was glad he had bought the gun. He believed his wife, who had previously frowned on what she called "Roger's new toy," was glad as well.

Life for Roger proceeded much as it had before the

gun purchase, until just the night before. He and his wife had forsaken generally bad TV for a good book.

"What was that?" his wife asked.

"What was what?" said Roger, looking up from his book.

"Probably nothing, but it sounded like something at the door."

Not only had Roger been hyper-sensitized by his self-defense seminar and the lurid newspaper stories of late, but he was also halfway through an Elmore Leonard novel. Warning bells went off in his head.

As he moved swiftly and steadily – for an old man – toward the front door, Roger took his gun from the lamp table beside his chair. Of late, he had taken to leaving the porch light on at night. So now there was some visibility through the peephole in the door. Peering into the night, he noted movement at the periphery of the lighted area of his yard. As his eyes adjusted, he could make out a figure – someone dressed in dark clothes, probably a man.

Well, Roger ol' fella, he thought as his pulse rate jumped perceptibly. *This looks like the showdown.*

"Call 9-1-1," he hissed at his wife.

No answer, then: "What am I going to tell them? You call 9-1-1."

That answer in these circumstances did not make Roger happy. *She's probably right, however*, he thought. *"I think I see a man standing at the edge of my yard" probably wouldn't get a cop to his house. After all, whoever it was was pretty close to the sidewalk. Didn't he have a right to be on the sidewalk?*

Reluctantly, Roger returned to his seat explaining that somebody was out there, but just on the sidewalk. "Probably out for an evening stroll. He'll probably go away if we ignore him."

Settling back to his book, reading was out of the question. Instead, the thoughts flooded in: *If he's on the sidewalk, what was the noise at the door? Why is he wearing all black? Isn't this what the guy meant when he said, "If it feels wrong, it probably is."* And *"Don't wait for it to happen to you."* Roger put his book down and went to the door.

This time when he looked, he could clearly see a man with dark hair dressed in black or very dark clothes. He was now easily in Roger's yard and seemed to be approaching the porch. Backing away from the door, Roger realized his hand holding the gun was beginning to sweat. In fact, Roger's forehead also began to sweat and his heart rate accelerated even more. Roger swallowed hard. He could wait or he could seize the initiative.

"What do you want?" Roger shouted, as he flung open the door and leveled the pistol.

"I just wanted to use your phone, sir," the man said. "My car's broken down there around the corner and yours is the only light on." The man slowly continued to move toward the house and Roger could see he was a young man, maybe a teenager, but bigger than Roger.

That sounds reasonable, Roger thought. *Just some kid whose car broke down – trying to call his folks, maybe.* Roger began to step back, as if to provide entry.

"Roger, don't let that man in here. We don't know who he might be." The voice of wifely wisdom from the doorway.

Instinctively, Roger knew she was right as he moved back toward the door. The man moved with him. Then Roger noticed the man's right hand. It was holding a club. Roger emptied the gun, which he still held leveled at the torso of the approaching figure in black.

*****

Roger had told Officer Mike the whole story when he arrived at the house with the MICU, but now Officer Mike was asking Roger to repeat the story. Of course, Roger hadn't mentioned the part about the self-defense seminar or the Elmore Leonard novel, but he had noted the series of home invasions he had read about in the newspaper as he recounted the night's events.

Finally he was finished. He paused a long while, then asked the question that had been bothering him. "Is the guy dead?"

"Yeah, he's dead, Roger. Five dum-dum .38s in the chest'll do it almost every time."

"Oh." Roger paused. "Now what happens?"

"Well, right now I'm gonna ask one of the officers to give you a ride home. After that, I don't really know. The DA will take a look at it. Decide whether to take it to the grand jury or not. If he doesn't, that's it. If he does, well, maybe they'll indict, maybe they won't. If they do, could be anything from negligent homicide to murder. Just can't say at this point."

Roger waited pensively, then asked, "Do you think I did the wrong thing? He was coming at me with a club. If he'd gotten close enough, no telling what he might have done. He might have killed me and my wife. I'm too old to fight barehanded."

"Well, it's not up to me. I just file the report." Officer Mike's voice was noncommittal.

When his transport officer arrived, Roger got up to leave. But then he had a second thought. "Eh, you found the club, didn't you?"

"Yeah. It was actually a tire tool, though. And there *was* a car parked around the block. Don't know who it belongs to yet."

"Oh," Roger said.

RULES OF THE ROAD

In my home state of Texas, we have, or at least we used to have, a small pamphlet for beginning drivers. It's called *The Rules of the Road*. For teenagers, committing this booklet to memory is just one more unpleasant thing that must be done before achieving freedom. However, that's not what it really is. What it is is a book of rules that allows the beginning driver to have a chance of moving from this place to that place in a motor vehicle with improved odds of bypassing a permanent stop at the morgue.

For the veteran automobile driver, *The Rules* is almost a matter of common sense. Fundamental things like: "Drive on the right side of a two-way street." "This is not a contest." "Pedestrians are a protected group. If you run over them, it's your fault." "Stop for solid things – even if you do have the right-of-way." Things like that.

"So what?" you ask. "Is this a documentary?"

No. It occurred to me that in this country, we have lots of rules to help us get through things that are new to us – at least get us started until we get the hang of it. I mean, if you want to make a nuclear bomb, all you need to do is go on the internet, google "things that go boom," and up pops detailed guidelines. Even pencil sharpeners come with instructions in three languages detailing just how it works and how to avoid injury when using it.

However, one of the most important things that every person in the United States, or anywhere else for that matter, will experience only once – as a total novelty – has no rules or guidelines or instructions. Old age.

As a matter of fact, we don't even know when old age starts anymore. (We know pretty well when it ends.) So for most of us – me, at least – we move along losing a faculty here and a faculty there without paying much attention. And then one day it happens: we get a card in the mail from AARP extending an invitation to join. (*"AARP! That's for old people. What do they want with me?"*)

Up until then, the denial process has shielded our feelings of worth and power. How many of us have stretched our arms until our shoulder almost popped out of joint because "they're making the print smaller"? Cut our hair just a little differently because it's "more stylish"? (*Thank you, Bruce Willis.*) Bought pants with an expandable waistband just because they're "more comfortable"?

But then the card comes and you know that at least somebody in authority thinks you are a "senior." And it's time to admit that you're no spring chicken anymore.

Still, although you might have lost a step or two, you are still the man/woman you always have been. Up goes a modified shield of denial and off you go again.

At some point thereafter, you begin to think of retirement... some day. And those stupid commercials about the golden years don't look so bad. Oddly those thoughts come and go with your job satisfaction.

One day you look up at the clock and it's damn close to striking midnight. Someone asks what plans you've made for retirement and reminds you that there's just a year or two until it's time. Then time blurs to a blink and there you are: walking out of your retirement party with a pension in one hand (if you're lucky) and a box full of accumulated stuff from your desk. Now what?

Well, if you've got the means, there's traveling to the places you've always wanted to see. Golf, lots of golf. But what about the time in between? What exactly is your role now?

If fortune has smiled and you have a close extended family, you have ol' Grampa Mudfrick to model after. (But he was a farmer.) If not, there's the years and years of TV examples. Amos McCoy comes to mind. Maud. (But those were sitcoms. This is the real deal.)

Again you say "So what? I've lived all my life. Just because I'm sixty-something doesn't mean I don't know how to be me. What's the problem?"

In a way, you're right. Being older and out of the job market doesn't change all the rules. The problem is that it changes some of the rules unless you're perfectly content to be marginalized. You know marginalized: people thinking this is the modern world and that an old guy/lady doesn't count or fit in.

It's a learning process, though. And if you work at it, you can make yourself relevant. The problem is, it's like learning to drive a car. You don't *have* to take lessons or read the rules. Just jump in and go. If you live long enough, you'll be a pretty good driver some day.

(We could do the same thing with teenagers, but we'd lose more of them than we already do. We don't want that, although I'm not sure why sometimes. So we give them *The Rules of the Road* to avoid it.)

If we had rules for aging, it would sure make getting old more pleasant. We could call them *Rules for the Retired* or (gag) *Golden Rules*. Toward that end, here are some suggestions for your golden years.

Rule 1: Don't retire.

I know. You're saying "Whada you, crazy?!? I've put in forty years at this job. Getting up at five in the morning, fighting my way through rush-hour traffic to get to a place where I'm not appreciated by the dipstick who's my boss. I do all the work and he gets all the credit. When it comes raise time, I get a lousy __% (Fill in the blank.) and he gets a huge bonus. Two crummy weeks of vacation. Thirty minutes for lunch. A desk that's older than I am and a secretary who's older and crustier than the desk." Or some variation. "Now I want to quit. Take it easy. Go places. Play golf. Sleep 'til the sun comes up. And live out the rest of my life in peace and harmony. I deserve that."

Let me tell you something my dad told me. "You can't play hooky if you don't go to school." I didn't know what it meant, either. But I do now. All the stuff you thought would be wonderful fun while you were dukin' it out with the real world isn't that much fun when it's what you do every day. What's the fun of playing golf when golf is functionally your job? You think Tiger Woods goes golfing for fun on his vacations?

I retired to the beach, and if I ever meet Jimmy Buffett, I'm gonna punch him in the nose. I think the reason Jimmy Buffett weaves his musical beach fantasies is because he is so busy writing songs and playing one concert after the other that he thinks retiring to the beach would be great, too.

Believe me, after putting forty years in the race, six months into the idles of retirement will begin to drive you right up a wall. Then you have the option of either just fading away while CNN tells you what to think or finding another job. And guess what? You're gonna have to start all over at the bottom at the new job with a brand new dipstick for a boss.

There's always volunteerism. But you're gonna have that same dipstick telling you what to do, and at the end of the day, your salary and your raise is bupkis. Then you're really gonna feel used.

And then there's the social aspect. You will soon find that you and the working world have little in common. The people you chat with at parties are going to get bored pretty fast when you start singing the glories of your wonderful shot on the ninth hole. And envy tends to bring things to a halt when you begin to regale people with your adventures in Spain. Soon you'll notice the invitations taper off and stop. That leaves you with those similarly situated. Not bad, but limiting and not exactly like dealing with the fully engaged.

If you happen to be single, "Hi. I'm an old fat bald guy on a fixed income" will not get you the romance you may or may not be able to handle. Likewise "I'm a frumpy old broad on a fixed income looking for a meal ticket" does little to arouse the passions of the opposite sex.

"Hold on," you say. "I already retired." Or "At my place, you're out at sixty-five – even if you're made of gold." That brings us to Rule 2.

Rule 2: If you are retired, never tell anyone.

There's a physical reaction you can observe when you meet new people who are still working and tell them you're retired. You can actually see their eyes glaze over. That physical manifestation mirrors the subconscious checklist of the person you're meeting: *This person is retired. Interesting? No. Important to my career? No. If I kiss him, he might turn into a handsome prince? No. Has a lot of money and will buy me things? Probably not. I think I'll go get another drink? Yes.*

The lesson here is, if you insist on subjecting yourself to rejection by the working world, wear a lot of bling. It's about the only thing that will get you somewhere you might want to go.

"So, I should lie?" you ask.

No. They'll discover the truth sooner or later and then it'll be worse. What you need is your old job back or a quasi-job that's interesting.

Putting aside the chance that you'll get your old job back because it's not gonna happen, and being a greeter at Walmart won't work as a quasi-job, there are other alternatives. A circumnavigator, a writer, a motorcycle racer, or an explorer/adventurer may get the job done.

"But wait," you say. "How can you just suddenly be one of those things? Or are we talking the ever useful white lie here?"

Well, paraphrasing a former president, what do you mean by "white"? Did you know that white is actually the blending of all the colors in the color spectrum? In any case, I'd like to think of a career as a broadly defined concept.

Let me tell you about a writer – since that's what I am. Writers come in all sizes and shapes and run the gamut from John Grisham to Maudie Fricker next door who is just starting to write her memoirs on used grocery sacks. Just because John sells gazillions of books that are made into movies and everybody knows his name, you can't say that Maudie, whose pencil scribblings will never see the light of day, is not a writer.

And if you really want to get ahead of the curve, write something and pay some printer to print it. Presto! You're a published writer.

Then when you go to a party and someone asks you "What do you do?" – instead of watching this person evaporate into bored disinterest when you say "I'm retired" – you can say, "I'm a writer." At this point, the person will say

"Oh." That means: *Hey, there's potential here.* But then the next question comes just like I'm telling you it will: "Are you published?" "Not yet" will work, but it's pretty lame. Everybody who has the time (the retired) is starting to write a book. A much more satisfactory answer is "Why, yes I am. Have you ever read (interesting title) by Lasloe Striker? That's my pen name." (A little wink.)

Now you're cookin'. Mr. or Ms. Potentially Right may or may not want to discuss literature with you, but the important thing is he or she has defined you as someone who may be of value instead of yesterday's news.

Later, after you have established that, retired or not, you're a fascinating human being, you can reveal the extent of your literary prowess. Either that, or pretend to be writing in your room while napping.

Rule 3: Don't ever go to the hospital.

Darrell Royal, the legendary Hall of Fame football coach at the University of Texas, speaking of the merits of the running game over the passing game, said "There are three things that can happen when you throw a pass. And two of 'em are bad."

That's a lot like going to the hospital: You can get better, you can get worse, or you can die. In other words, when you check into the hospital, you've got a two-out-of-three chance of something happening that's bad.

I can't cite the national census or *The World Atlas*, but let's fall back on common sense. Comparing the general population with the hospital population, who do you think experiences the higher incidence of death?

People die everywhere, but your odds of dying go way up in the hospital. And the older you are, the worse your odds get.

"Harhay," you say. "You're playing fast and loose with statistics."

Well, maybe, but look at it from the good side. Say you go to the hospital and after a while you get better and leave. In the meantime, what happens?

Step number one is when the compassionate nurse hands you a stack of documents to sign releasing from liability the hospital, doctor, nurse, orderly, administrative staff, and anyone near, or who might be near, the hospital who might in some way cause you harm.

Step number two is when the compassionate nurse

puts you on a gurney and sticks a long needle, which is attached to a mystery bag, in a vein in your arm. This is not like having your foot cut off, but it's not comfortable. Who knows what's in the bag or why they do it? I had always assumed that the bag had some kind of knock-out stuff in it, but it doesn't and they don't tell you what *is* in it. You just lay there awake, perhaps in pain, with a bag attached to a needle in your arm and mostly naked.

Way later, the doctor enters. At this point, it's either lights out, or poking and thumping and more needles. If the former, very shortly in your mind, you wake up and leave with a lot less money than you had when you walked in. If the latter, you are directed to go see a specialist who will take even more of your money.

If in fact you were subjected to "a procedure," leaving the hospital is when the fun really begins. In times past, it was called pain and torture. Now it's called rehabilitation, and it goes on forever, or until something bad happens and you have to go back into the hospital where the whole fun thing starts over again.

Still doubtful? Let's just say you elected not to go to the hospital. What would happen?

Odds are you'd get better. The human body, even an old human body, has an incredible capacity to heal itself with a little rest, especially if you stop doing whatever it was that caused the problem in the first place.

Rule 4: You are not as good as you ever were. Behave.

I am not, NOT, saying grow old gracefully. What I'm saying is you're old. Your body – all the muscles, organs, and all the little neurons – has been cranking 24/7 for sixty-something years. In that time period, if you had a full life, you may have subjected your body to various toxins or activities that taxed it more than normal. As a result of all that living, your body is tiring and slowing down. You must gauge your activities accordingly, despite your irrational but strongly held belief that you're just as good as you ever were. Trust me. You're not.

You cannot think as quickly, move as fast, lift as much, see as clearly, hear as sharply, taste as acutely, or have sex as often. (You will have to pee more often, though.) If you disregard Rule 4, you will hurt or embarrass yourself. To avoid this, you must be aware of your limitations and act accordingly.

Let's use me as an illustration.

I've always been what people call an exercise nut. Throughout life, the only thing that kept me from exercising more was the need to eat, sleep, and earn a living. When I retired, that freed up at least eight more hours a day. For some odd reason, I decided I actually had the body of the twenty-something I still was in my head.

In psychiatry, this situation would be characterized as psychosis – a clear break with reality.

More biking, skiing, jogging, and lifting weights – all with the vigor of a twenty-something. In my mind, I would become some weird combination of Lance Armstrong, Jean Claude Killey, Jim Fixx, and Arnold Swartzenegger. I would trim myself into a superperson who would potentially live forever.

What I actually did was pretty much destroy me. I now have knees in need of daily icing and periodic draining, a shoulder that required rotator cuff surgery, and a back that seems to randomly decide that I should lie on the floor for a week or so.

You would think a sixty-something would know better. In fact, I think being sixty-something actually exacerbates the problem, but in any case, nobody had warned me. So let me warn you.

The rule of thumb is: "Take it slow and if it hurts stop doing it." That, and get your head right – elite athletes are *not* sixty-something. "No pain, no gain" is somebody's sadistic fantasy.

"So, what if I'm not an exercise fanatic?" you ask. "Scratch the rule?"

No. It's not just an exercise thing, even if the definition of exercise is broad enough to include such activities as dancing and love-making. The rule of mentally conforming "then" with "now" applies to lots of things.

Eating, for instance. You can no longer eat two bacon cheeseburgers and fries with your six-pack of beer. It may take your metabolism weeks to burn one French fry, one bite of cheeseburger, and one beer. And that says nothing of the grief greasy fried chicken may cause your diminished stomach lining at night.

Or driving. Your grandson may be able to text message, listen to his iPod, check out the attractive lady jogger, and still react quickly enough to avoid the idiot in front of him who just stopped for no reason. At sixty-something, you better save the extracurricular activities for when you get home. The little neurons just don't fire as fast as they used to.

Rule 5: Fight world shrink.

"Do what?" you ask.

I know you understand "fight." So you must be wondering about "world shrink."

It's a term I'm using to describe a peculiar thing that happens when people get older. A person's world – the places that are experienced on a day-to-day, week-to-week, or year-to-year basis – actually shrinks.

Let's say when you were young, you wanted to join the Navy to see the world. So you did, going from one exciting location to another seeking whatever adventure it might offer. At some point, you probably left the Navy and got a job in some city. You then explored that city and went on vacation to all sorts of places. Along with the physical world, you explored the interpersonal world – had experiences with different people. Some of the experiences were good, some were bad, but you continued to explore what was out there because you were curious. Somewhere along the way, you probably married and had children, and then you included your family in your adventures so that you could all share them.

Sometime after your kids left home, or maybe after your kids had kids, you found yourself saying things like "I think this year I'm just gonna hang around the house for a vacation – do things I've been putting off." Or "Go to the football game? I like it better on TV." Or "Why would I go out to eat? The food I fix at home is always better." Or "I'm sick of being disturbed by the phone. I think I'll get it turned off." Eventually, you only leave your home to go to the doctor's office or the grocery store. Your experiential world has compacted from the planet Earth to three or four rooms in some city.

You are the victim of world shrink, and unless you want to spend your golden years being terrorized by the TV prophets of political apocalypse, it's something upon which you must actively make war. It's insidious but, on the surface, it's reasonable, and it creeps up on you until before you know it, it's got you cornered in front of the TV. So, like waging war, you must know your enemy and have a battle plan that you execute faithfully.

Regardless of what you tell yourself, what's happening

is that as your faculties fade, you recognize, perhaps subconsciously, that the uncertainties of life are more difficult to deal with. This is true, and you may, in fact, be much more comfortable with the limited challenges offered by your four rooms. If you understand the process and will it to be so, then so be it.

On the other hand, if you're not really content seeing the incredible richness of life diminish to whatever is on TV, you must fight it. When the opportunity arises for going out in the world, conversely to Nancy Reagan's advice on premarital sex, or maybe it was drugs, just say "yes." And as the population ages, there are tours geared for seniors to just about any place you might want to go. Pick a place and go.

I mean, how bad could it possibly be? You get trampled in the buffet line? Consider the alternative: death by reality TV.

Rule Last: The omnibus rule: Always plan for booger.

Murphy was, in my opinion, a genius. His law specifies that if anything bad can happen, it will happen.

My father, a latent philosopher, said, "Always plan for booger."

Whereas Murphy was suggesting the certainty of possible disruptions, Dad was talking about planning alternate courses of action in advance to avoid Murphy's consequences. I, being your basic kid, thought "booger" was just a funny word.

In later life, I would come to see the truth in Dad's Corollary to Murphy's Law. Let me now add an addendum to Dad's Corollary. It is a progressive rule. That is to say, the older you get, the more truth it embodies.

What I mean is, at younger ages, people have the time and the physical capacity to react to more and varied problems they encounter. With age, of course, comes wisdom – the "I've seen this situation before and this is what you can do to deal with it" kind of wisdom. With age also comes a lower frustration tolerance, slower reaction time, and less actual time to correct an error. In youth, a person has the time to try lots of different alternatives and the capacity to do it relatively quickly.

"So what are you trying to say?" you ask.

My point is that in later years, you need to use the advantage that wisdom gives by planning in advance for things that might happen, so you can deal with them to your benefit.

An easy example. You're going to Hawaii for your umpteenth golf vacation. Be that as it may, you would still like to get there. Your plane leaves at noon. It takes one hour to get to the airport. Two hours to deal with the ticket line, fight your way through security, and get on the plane. What time do you leave home?

That's easy. One and two makes three: nine o'clock in the morning. But youngsters are optimists, so they fudge and leave at ten.

At this point, wisdom may tell you to give up and play your home course. It's not worth the trouble. However, if you do choose to go, you know there are the potential time eaters of rush-hour traffic, flat tires, weather, and somebody in front of you in the ticket line who's trying to buy plane tickets with frequent flyer points for Toronto routed through Amsterdam, Iceland, and China – what Dad would have called booger factors.

So you leave even thirty minutes earlier. That way, the worst thing (reasonably foreseeable) that can happen is you end up spending thirty minutes in the bar waiting for your flight to board.

Obviously, booger may come in many different forms

and in many different pursuits. I could stretch this by trying to name them, but you get the point. At sixty-something, you know that lots of things can happen that might keep you from doing what you want to do. Know your limitations. Use your experience. Plan ahead. Avoid the difficulties.

In fact, maybe that's what all the "rules toward the end of the road" boil down to – if you add in enjoying every day of whatever life allows and loving those who love you.

DEATH AND TAXES

"Hello," he said. "You're Arthur Wascom."

He was right about that. But who was he? And why
was he out here on the beach? It was fall on the Gulf of Mexico, which meant bathing suits and tank tops, or just bathing
suits. The man addressing me was in full business regalia –
white shirt, power tie, dark blue suit, and wing-tips. Even if it
weren't for the heat, no local would wear a suit on the beach.
Heck, by now both wing-tips were probably half-full of sand.
Soon his neatly coiffed black hair would be blown sky-west
and crooked.

"Yep. Have been all my life." I eyed him, letting just
the noise of the lightly breaking waves engulf us.

"You're seventy years old," he said, deciding, I guess,

that I wasn't going to say anything else if he didn't.

"Right again, young feller." He wasn't really all that young – maybe late forties or early fifties – but I added that last part to let him know who's who.

He smiled. "I'm a lot older than I look."

Again, the only sound was that of the waves. But this time I blinked first, so to speak. "Can I help you?"

"Yes, I think so," he said and stopped.

I waited. "Well, you're gonna have to tell me how. Don't do well at mind readin'."

"Perhaps," he began again, "I should introduce myself. People call me Death." Clearly he thought that would get a reaction, and it did.

"Ha," I laughed, thinking *People ought to call you a nut.*

He looked a little disappointed. "No. It's true – the Grim Reaper, the Angel of Death, other things over the years. Oddly, I'm not sure why or how they might know. Usually the only time a person ever sees me, I'm the last thing he sees." He paused, allowing me to consider what he'd just said. "In just a few minutes, you're going to feel some tightness in your chest, and seconds after that, you'll be gone. Actually you won't be gone. You'll be right here, but then you'll come with me and we'll be gone. I'm like your escort," he said with a head flip that displayed his distaff side.

Now here was something that didn't happen every day. I've seen a lot of strange sorts on this beach, but this was a first. Being a little flustered by the situation, I said the first thing that popped into my mind. "You got some ID?"

Now it was his turn to laugh. "For the time being, you don't have to believe me if you don't want to. In just a little bit, you'll have all the evidence you need."

"Well, I don't – believe you that is – but if I did, why would you be here talkin' to me? I mean, why not step in afterwards? Save yourself some grief." This guy was kinda creepin' me out.

"Oh, believe me, I won't feel grief. When you've done this as long as I have, seeing a person die is sort of like watching a bad soap opera. I know the end and how it's going to happen. How many death scenes do you think there could possibly be?"

"I didn't really mean grief, like grief. It's a term we use to mean 'save yourself some bother.'"

"Oh. Well, it's no bother, either. It's my job. In fact, the reason I do it this way is to add a little variety. You know, meet the person. See what he's like 'before.' 'After' everybody is about the same – 'Where am I going? Is heaven a neat place? Can I go back and visit? I always tried to be good.' Yada, yada, same ol', same ol'. So I take a little time to chat when my client might actually have something interesting to say."

Curiouser and curiouser, I thought. "Mr. Death," I said, giving him my most serious and sympathetic look. "Do you have some family or friends I can call? You see, I know you believe what you're telling me, but – no offense meant – I don't. And it's been my experience that when some things just don't add up, it's likely… eh, not entirely the truth."

At that, the man looked downright haughty. "I think you're just a cynic. Sure, this whole thing is a little unusual, but how would you expect it to play out? Why do you think I'm out here in a suit? Look at me. I'm not even sweating. Suit's not rumpled. Hair is perfect, if I do say so myself." He raised his hands and looked around, as if to say "What else could it be?"

"Look. I don't mean to offend you, but you could be anybody. Well… you could be any strange person. This could be some sort of club initiation: 'If you can convince some ol' guy you're the Angel of Death, we'll let you in our club' kinda thing. I just don't believe it. Sorry," I said, a little bit more confidently than I felt.

He took a deep breath and closed his eyes for a moment. "What would it take to convince you?"

That gave me pause. "I don't know. Can you do magic, supernatural tricks? Maybe if you could disappear all of a sudden and then come back?"

"I can't disappear right now. When I disappear, I have to take you with me. This may seem random to you, but there are some rules." He seemed frustrated.

"All right," I said, hoping that he couldn't convince me. "Do you know stuff that only you could know?" That was how they did it on the TV cop shows.

He thought about that. "If only I could know it, how would you know if it was something only I could know?"

"Hmm." He had a point. "Maybe something only you and I could know?"

"You mean like things you did in your life? Secret things?"

"Yeah," I said. "But not too personal. Just something… secret – like where I buried my pet lizard when I was a kid."

"I can't do that sort of thing. My job is to escort people to the afterlife when they die. I don't have the omniscient brain thing."

"Mmm," I grunted.

We both frowned in thought.

"Hey!" I brightened. "I just thought of something. You say your job is to escort people when they die, right?"

He nodded.

"Well, how do you do that? I mean, there must be thousands of people that die every second, and you've been standing here talking to me for fifteen minutes or so."

"Oh, I see." He smiled. "If people are dying right now and my job is to escort them, but I'm standing here in front of you, either I'm not doing my job or I'm lying." He paused. "You realize we're working backwards here. We're supposed to be establishing that I am who I say I am, not that I'm lying about it. Be that as it may, it's really pretty simple. Although I could be just goofing off, the rules don't allow that, and there's hell to pay for breaking the rules. No, the fact of the matter is I can be in many places at the same time."

"Aw, bullshit," I exclaimed before I could stop myself. "I mean… that's really hard to believe."

He shrugged. "Well, here we go again. But you see, when you're celestial, being in several places at once is not really very hard. It's a dimensional thing. On the other hand, it's a little like understanding the nature of God. Maybe you really have to be there." He thought for a bit. "OK. Ask me a question, a really hard one."

"How many angels can dance on the head of a pin?" I fired back. It's something I'd been thinking about.

"None," he replied thoughtfully. "Angels are great big beings. If an angel tried to dance on the head of a pin, he'd prick his foot."

As I looked him in the eyes, I could see the same recognition he probably saw in mine. To believe he was telling the truth, I'd have to believe he knew how big an angel was. This bootstrapping approach to the truth just wasn't working. He knew it and I knew it. I wondered if that made any difference.

"Mr. Wascom," he said.

"Call me Artie. Everybody does," I said, interrupting.

"Artie, I've never had this problem before. What I

mean is, until the last several years, people were always pretty content to accept me as Death, have a nice little chat, and go on about our business. Now, in the last twenty years or so, and especially in this country, people won't believe I'm who I say I am. Of course, 'after' I get to say 'Told you so,' but that's not as good as having the chat 'before.' Who wants to have a chat with somebody who's giving you his best pitch to stay out of hell? Then they won't believe me when I tell them I've got no juice with the Decider. What is the problem here?"

"For what it's worth – I mean, I'm no expert – I don't think people trust anybody anymore. I sure don't. And this particular situation is even a little beyond the everyday stuff. So it's not too difficult to figure people are not believin' you when you show up in a suit claimin' to be the Angel of Death. At least you could have wings or something."

"But why now? Why all of a sudden?" Death seemed to be genuinely interested.

I tried to explain. "For the record, 'twenty years or so' isn't all of a sudden... at least in human time. But back to the point, it seems to me that sometime – I didn't much notice it at first – truth took the big one and went elsewhere."

Death kind of screwed up his nose and made a face as if he'd bitten into a lemon.

"It's a concept, a manner of speaking," I said. "Truth didn't really die; it just seemed to be absent one day. It was like somebody or a bunch of somebodies were in a bind and realized that it wasn't the truth of a thing that mattered, it was saying the thing was the truth that would get you what you wanted."

"I'm not tracking you here, Artie. Help me," he said.

"I don't guess you've ever been divorced." I gave him an expectant look. He scrunched up his nose. "Didn't think so. OK, another example. Let's say you want to build a big ol' hotel right here on the beach. You know it's gonna kill the natural beauty and create traffic problems and such. So when you ask the government if it's OK, you tell 'em about all the jobs it'll create and the tax revenue it'll bring in. And instead of saying the big ol' thing will look like shit, you say the architecture will enhance the cosmopolitan image of the area. See?"

"You're saying people lie to get what they want, right? Not new, Artie. Been going on since Eve told Adam it was just an apple."

"Yeah, I know, but that's just part of it. Everybody knows that people will lie to get what they want, and when you know they want something, you just kinda assume they're lyin' to get it. But once upon a time, it always seemed that there was something to give you a clue that you might be being lied to. You know, like watchdog newspapers, ministers, honest politicians."

At that, Death smirked. "Sorry. 'Honest politician.' Couldn't help it."

"See. You don't even remember. Once there was such a thing."

"Oh, you mean like elves and fairies?" Death smirked again.

"OK. Take that one off the list. But you understand what I mean, like guideposts to help you know what was true and what wasn't. Then somehow everybody got in the game. Everybody had some agenda that was a lot more important than the truth. So all of a sudden, the only one you could be pretty sure wasn't lyin' to you was your momma... if she didn't want something." I swallowed hard and collected myself. "The words 'authoritative source' used to mean someone who knew the truth. Now it doesn't mean anything. It could mean someone who ought to know the truth, but will happily spin it to promote his own agenda. Or it could be just a writing technique – something the writer threw in to make what he's saying sound more convincing. Large elephants are routinely hidden behind small feathers. Words have become almost valueless except in a contrarian sense. Like the old joke: 'How do you know when a lawyer is lying? When his lips are moving.' Now if someone is telling you something, it's safer to assume the opposite is true. Nothin's for sure anymore."

"Hmm," Death said, putting his index finger across his lips and peering out at the gulf. "Perhaps truth has its own unique form of 'ID' as you say." Death hesitated for a minute longer, then continued. "So, you see? The little chat was interesting and worthwhile, but now it's that time."

All of a sudden, I realized two things for sure. *This guy isn't spoofin' me. It's prove-up time and he's fixin' to prove it. And I'm not ready to go anywhere with anybody out of this life.*

"Wait a minute," I said, beginning to seriously sweat. "You said something about rules." I was grasping at straws, but he refocused his attention.

"Yes, I did. Why?"

"Doesn't it say somewhere, in a big book or somethin', that I was supposed to be taken about thirty minutes ago?"

"Yes, it does," Death agreed.

"And didn't you say that breaking the rules is a big no-no at your shop?"

He smiled, but let me continue.

"So if you took me now, that would be against the rules, right? So you can't do it." I was amazed at my logic. All those years of watching Captain Kirk argue with computers on *Star Trek* weren't wasted after all.

"Interesting… but not fascinating." He winked.

Something in my chest began to feel odd.

RETIREMENT INCOME

The big hand on the oversized wall clock indicated that very soon the bailiff would stand and announce "The criminal district court is now in session – the Honorable Freeman Porterfield presiding. God bless America and this honorable court." But right now, the bailiff was sitting off to the left at his desk working a crossword puzzle, oblivious to the fact that my world might well be coming to an end.

Don't misunderstand. I wasn't charged with a capital crime carrying the death penalty. It was just that, at my age, any term in jail probably meant a life sentence for me. I wouldn't fare well in prison for any length of time.

On my right, beside me at counsel table, sat Shepherd Masters, my lawyer. He was an excellent criminal lawyer, but at the moment he was busily playing with his iPhone – either figuring out how much money he was losing while we waited or checking his missed messages.

At the other counsel table sat a terrible bitch named Linda Lou Atkins. Linda Lou was the prosecutor.

Shepherd had explained that Linda Lou really didn't hate me. "She's just doing her job," he said.

I, however, thought he was wrong. Linda Lou had an aura of pure mean emanating generally from her presence, but focused exclusively on me for the time being.

The jury had been out for three days, but had finally signaled the bailiff about an hour ago that it had reached a decision.

Shepherd had told me that the longer the jury stayed out, the better it was for me. It meant the jurors were having trouble deciding my punishment. Of course, Shepherd had also told me earlier that the jury would have a great deal of sympathy for a man my age and would very likely find me not guilty. That was wrong. After the judge read the charge explaining the crime with which I was charged and what the prosecution had to prove, it took them all of ten minutes to go out, elect a foreperson, vote, and come back "guilty." So I hoped Shepherd was right this time. It had been way over ten minutes.

A week ago, I had entered this peculiar place called the criminal district court, confident that, even though I might have been technically guilty, no jury would find a nice old guy like me guilty for merely trying to make some additional money in bad economic times. I had visions of moonshiners in West Virginia; Jesse James fighting the ruthless railroad; or *Boston Legal*, the TV show.

However, my confidence began to ebb during the jury selection process when the Honorable Porterfield expounded on the jury's responsibility. He never mentioned economic hard times or nice old guys at all. I had not thought the sword of blind justice was quite so keen.

The ebb of confidence caused by the judge turned into an outward flood when Linda Lou got her turn. She said that sympathy had no place at trial and anyone who might think it did couldn't be on the jury. She had a very irritating habit of glaring at me when she mentioned the word "criminal" or noted that lots of people are in fact guilty despite the presumption to the contrary. By the time Linda Lou finished,

I doubted that there was a single potential juror left with one iota of sympathy.

Fortunately, Shepherd got to speak as well. This was much better. He emphasized my age and lack of a criminal record. He dwelled on the very, very high standard of proof. Standing on his tiptoes and reaching as high as possible to touch that imaginary standard, he proclaimed that the jury could not find me guilty unless the prosecutor proved beyond all reasonable doubt that I was guilty. He spoke a little about the concept of jury nullification, a process by which the jury can simply decide not to follow an unjust law, before Linda Lou cut him off with an objection. It seems it's not cricket to ask the jury to violate their oath.

When the dust cleared, we seated twelve people who looked pretty much like a cross-section of the community. I would have much preferred a bunch of sixty-something-year-old men on Social Security, but Linda Lou seemed to have excused almost all of them. I took solace in the fact that the jury wasn't completely composed of Young Republicans.

The trial started and it was the prosecutor's time to present evidence. Her first witness was a fatherly-looking guy who identified himself as Sergeant Seamus McGuire of the

Drug Interdiction Division with twenty-five years of police experience. Included in that twenty-five years was fourteen courses on drug offenses, drug identification, identification of the paraphernalia used to produce illegal drugs, and the societal impact of illegal drugs on the youth of our country. Sergeant McGuire spoke with a pleasant authoritative baritone. His sad eyes suggested that he had no personal animosity toward me, but the law had to be followed or our society would collapse into Sodom or Gomorrah.

Through a process of question and answer, Sergeant McGuire detailed how he had been contacted by an undercover vice cop, who advised that he had been approached by a person seeking to buy seeds to grow marijuana. Subsequently, Sergeant McGuire had obtained a warrant to search a residence "which I would later come to know was the residence of the defendant." He pointed the finger of guilt at me.

"And did you find anything that, from your experience, you could identify as paraphernalia used in the manufacture and sale of drugs? And, if so, what did you find?" Linda Lou sneered in my direction.

"Why, yes I did," Sergeant McGuire said like it was some kind of a surprise. "In the basement, I found twenty large pots, ten bags of fertilizer, a light heating system, and provisions to divert water from the lawn sprinkler to the basement for watering the plants."

"And are these things illegal in and of themselves?" Linda Lou pitched the softball.

"No," said McGuire seriously. "But in my experience they are commonly used in the growing of illegal marijuana."

"And, again based on your experience in drug enforcement, what would this kind of setup produce?" Linda Lou asked, feigning genuine curiosity.

"Well," McGuire pensively tapped his lip, "around twenty pounds of high grade marijuana with a street value of over one hundred thousand dollars."

"And based on your knowledge, what would be the effect of the introduction of that much marijuana into our county?"

"Oh, it would have a devastating effect." McGuire looked at the jury with those sad eyes. "Most of it would undoubtedly fall into the hands of children and would be their first step to hard drugs and a life of crime."

"Awk!" I said a little too loud, drawing a hard look from the judge. "Is he crazy?"

Shepherd shushed me. It was his turn to ask the questions.

"Mr. McGuire," Shepherd began, taking care not to cloak McGuire with a title. "If you had decided that the farming implements found in my client's basement were for growing tomatoes, we wouldn't be here would we?"

"No." McGuire chuckled.

"In fact, wouldn't it be safe to say that, had your informant not pointed the finger at my client, the things you found in my client's basement would be equally fitted for growing marijuana or tomatoes?"

"Well… I guess that's true. I'm not an expert in growing tomatoes." McGuire did not wish to concede anything and drew polite laughter from the jury.

"But in truth, Mr. McGuire, there's no law against me, you, or the jury keeping pots, fertilizer, lights, and water in our basements?"

McGuire hesitated.

"That's what you told the prosecutor, isn't it?"

McGuire reluctantly confirmed Shepherd's statement.

"And tell us, if you know, did my client actually acquire marijuana seeds?"

"Eh… no he didn't."

After that, Shepherd called into question McGuire's unfounded statements regarding the amount of marijuana that would be produced and where, if any was produced, it might end up. Although we had no expert witness, Shepherd managed to poke fun at McGuire's assertion regarding the progress "to hard drugs and a life of crime" with a reference to the 1936 movie, *Reefer Madness.* The prosecutor objected, Shepherd withdrew the question, but the jury got the message.

Just before passing the witness back to the prosecutor, Shepherd made a *Columbo* move. "Oh, I almost forgot. Just one more question – just so the jury will understand. Is my information correct that you led ten black-clad men armed with automatic weapons in breaking down my client's front door? Then totally trashed his house… *after* you found the things the warrant allowed you to search for?"

McGuire reddened. "Well, we didn't know who was inside the house. It could have been a gang of Colombian drug-cartel killers."

At that response, Shepherd actually laughed. Then he deftly established that the undercover cop had described the potential purchaser as basically an old fat bald guy.

The prosecutor chose not to redirect.

The prosecutor's next witness was the undercover cop. I recognized him as the same scruffy little guy I had approached for marijuana seeds. It turned out that his real name was Freddy Rizzo, and he essentially told the truth: I had asked him if he could sell me some marijuana seeds suitable for growing marijuana.

We didn't have much to work with. However, before Rizzo left the witness stand, Shepherd did establish that Rizzo did, in fact, lie for a living. That is, it was his job to tell people that he was a drug dealer. Furthermore, neither money nor marijuana seeds changed hands between Rizzo and I.

That was the state's case. We could have rested right then and let the jury return a verdict on the evidence presented. That's what Shepherd suggested, and in retrospect, it may have been the thing to do. However, I was not convinced that, absent my testimony, we had had our "day in court." I wanted to tell my side. Shepherd called me to the stand.

"Tell us," he said, directing the question at me. "Are you a drug dealer?"

"No," I said truthfully. "I've never sold drugs in my

life." *I never got the chance*, I thought.

"What do you do?" he asked.

"I was laid off when my company went under and now I live on Social Security."

"Then you're over sixty-two?" he concluded.

"Actually sixty-seven," I corrected.

"Married?"

"No. Widowed."

"Children?"

"Two… and four grandchildren."

Shepherd tried to get off into my military service, but the judge sustained Linda Lou's objection to that one. After thinking a minute, he concluded, "Do you believe you are guilty of attempting to grow and sell illegal drugs?"

Of course I answered "No" because I didn't buy any seeds. And even if I had, I wasn't sure I could grow marijuana. And I sure didn't know how I might go about selling it if I *had* been successful in growing it.

Now the hellbitch fixed me with an evil stare, sneering as she began. "Were you gonna grow tomatoes?"

"Well, no," I answered. I didn't know how to grow tomatoes, either.

"Isn't it a fact that if Detective Rizzo had sold you marijuana seeds, you were gonna grow you some marijuana?" Linda Lou's sarcasm knew no bounds.

"No," I said weakly.

"Hmm?" Linda Lou made it sound like I had just answered in Japanese. "Are you telling us," she gestured to the jury, "that you had all the stuff to grow marijuana in your basement and you asked Detective Rizzo to sell you some marijuana seeds to grow marijuana, but you weren't really going to grow marijuana? Is that it?"

"Well, I'm not sure if I would have grown marijuana or not. I don't know if I really know how," I answered.

"Okey-dokey," she smirked, and then made her own *Columbo* move. "Oh, but you did buy all the marijuana-growing paraphernalia and you did ask Detective Rizzo to sell you some seeds to grow marijuana, right?"

"Yes, I guess so." I couldn't very well deny it. I was under oath.

"You 'guess' so?" She paused. "I'll take that as a 'yes.' Pass the witness."

Shepherd passed as well.

His Honor told the jurors they must return a verdict

of guilty if they believed beyond a reasonable doubt that I had attempted to buy marijuana seeds with the intent to grow and sell an illegal drug. "Attempt" meant something more than mere preparation. There must have been an overt act facilitating the commission of the crime. And an "illegal drug" included marijuana.

Shepherd argued that there was no more than mere preparation and tried as hard as he could to portray me as a sympathetic old man. Linda Lou argued that asking Rizzo to sell me the marijuana was the overt act, and concluded with a plea to stop the epidemic of drug crime that was ruining our children.

The jury went with door number two.

In the punishment phase of the trial, Shepherd could, and did, get into all sorts of things suggesting that the jury should have sympathy for me and be very lenient. He called my kids, my neighbors, my pastor, and my former employer as witnesses. They all said what a wonderful law abiding old guy I was. He pointed to the conspicuous absence of a criminal record, and introduced my military discharge and commendations into evidence. Linda Lou looked bored and didn't have much to say. I did not make the mistake of getting on that witness stand again. The jury already knew I was living on Social Security and the economy was bad. There wasn't much I could add.

Shepherd highlighted all the testimony in his final argument, patted me on the shoulder, and suggested that a short probation would best serve society and me. The jury looked noncommittal.

Linda Lou stood looking cranky. "You know, every criminal's got some excuse, but you found this guy," she pointed the long finger of guilt directly at me, "guilty of a major offense. I'll bet some of you have had some hard times, but you didn't go out and become a criminal to make some extra money. You know about the drug problem in this country. Now the question is what you're gonna do about it. You gonna slap him on the wrist and turn him loose? Or are you gonna do your duty and send a message to other drug criminals who would make a little extra money by sellin' drugs to our kids?"

Some of the jurors nodded.

Of all the parts of this whole thing, waiting for the jury to come back with my punishment was the worst. *Why*, I reasoned, *didn't they see that I was just a harmless old man trying to make ends meet in tough times? How could they possibly believe that I was a bad person? Didn't they understand that marijuana wasn't really a bad drug? Maybe they didn't see Reefer Madness? Maybe they were all "wing nut" conservatives? How could they end a man's life for just thinking about breaking the law?*

It was in this state of mind that I sought refuge from a higher court. *God*, I prayed silently but fervently, *if You'll get me out of this, I'll never do another bad thing in my life. I'll go back to church. I'll tithe. Oh, please have mercy on me. It was just a bad decision.*

As the jury filed into the jury box, only one elderly woman looked at me at all. I hoped what I saw in her eyes was sympathy. After the judge read the jury decision to himself, he passed the verdict form back to the foreperson to read. In the periphery of my vision, I saw Linda Lou smirk.

"Having found the defendant guilty of the offense of attempted production and sale of a dangerous drug, we now assess a penalty of ten years in prison."

That was it. The words hit me like a medicine ball in the stomach. What was left of my life would now be spent in some state prison as a "bitch" for someone called Big Mau-

rice. No more nice bed. No more TV. No more anything ap-
proximating freedom. As the tears rolled down my face, I
fainted.

When I re-entered the world of the living, Shepherd
was standing over me and the courtroom was clear. *Why am I
not in prison?* I wondered.

Shepherd patted my shoulder and helped me to my
feet. "It's gonna be OK," he reassured.

"How is ten years in prison OK?" I whimpered.

"You missed the rest of what the jury decided. After
'ten years in prison,' the jury foreperson said 'However, we
recommend that this sentence be suspended and the defendant be put on probation for a period of five years.'"

Deliverance, I thought. *Thank you, God.*

As I left the courtroom, I thanked Shepherd profusely
and smiled at Linda Lou – covertly giving her the finger.

It wasn't exactly a victory celebration, though. Shepherd explained that I would have to report to my probation
officer monthly and there would be a monthly probation fee
along with court costs, and, of course, my legal fees. I didn't
think it would be a problem for me to stay out of trouble. I
had managed that for sixty-seven years. But where I might get

any additional money was a mystery to me. I wondered how God might feel if I skipped the tithe – at least until I was off probation.

TRANSITIONS

"Bug," the man cried. Surprised at his own volume, he turned to see if anyone was close enough to hear.

He was an old man dressed in a dusty brown overcoat and matching hat from which cotton-gray hair protruded. He was sitting, stooped, on a park bench, studying the ground in front of him. At least that's what he appeared to be studying. In fact, he was appraising a small crawling insect.

This time, checking first for unwanted listeners, he shouted: "Bug."

The bug stopped his relentless progress to wherever bugs find it so imperative to go.

"Bug," the man said in a much more conversational tone. "Do you hear me?"

The bug, of course, said nothing, but he didn't move either.

"Well, bug, tell me," he said, as if the bug might actually speak. "Are you coming or going?"

Again, the bug did not respond... at least not vocally.

The old man again scanned for kibitzers, then considered picking the bug up and putting him in his hat. Thinking that through, he decided that it would look every bit as peculiar to be talking to your hat as to be talking to a bug. He continued as before.

"This may be a delicate question, but what I need to know is if you are somewhere in the reincarnation cycle."

The bug wiggled his back pincers, but said nothing.

"I suppose you could have been a very bad human in a former life. Come to think of it, you could have been a very good human in a former life. But we humans like to think of ourselves as the highest form of life on this planet. So I'm guessing you were a real scudder in your last life. Or you're working your way up from earthworm."

The bug again began his journey.

"No. Wait, bug. I didn't mean to offend you. I'm very serious. Please don't go."

The bug stopped.

"You see – I suppose you can see – I'm an old man. I've lived long, but now I believe I'm reaching the end of my life. I guess I should know this, but I don't. How long do bugs – your kind of bug, that is – live? Humans, the male ones, now live to be about seventy-seven years old. I'm eighty-four, so I'm due any day now. I was never much concerned about what happens after you die, but as time shortens, so to speak, I have become obsessed with the question of what comes next. I mean, do the lights just go out? Do you wake up in some lovely place where your every dream comes true? Do you go some place that's not so pleasant if you didn't do so well in this life? Does your life's energy go somewhere, regroup, and come back as something else somewhere else? Or maybe part of something else somewhere else?"

The bug shifted. The man realized he had come nearer to the bug as he became caught up in his quest.

"Maybe you're wondering why I'm asking you," the man said, leaning back. "Humans don't normally talk to bugs. But if you think about it, why should I ask another human? If we knew, I wouldn't have to ask anyone. Of course, a few humans believe they used to be Napoleon or Julius Caesar in another life, but usually we keep those humans away from the rest of us. If the lights just go out at the end and never come back on, then it doesn't matter who I ask. But if we actually come back in some other form, then asking another species makes sense."

The bug stilled as if waiting.

As the man prepared to continue, off to his right he heard, "Why, Mr. Jensen, what brings you to our park?"

The man immediately recognized Erma Floyd's voice. Erma Floyd was a lay minister at the church and she knew everything about everybody who lived in town. If she didn't, she made it her business to find out. As near as anyone could tell, finding out about other people's business *was* Erma Floyd's business.

Seeing several potential problems in the unexpected appearance of Erma Floyd, the man quickly dropped his hat over the bug. "Howdy, Erma," the man said.

"Oh, you dropped your hat," Erma exclaimed. "Let me get it for you."

As Erma moved in the general direction of the man's hat, the man extended his hand in a gesture of restraint. "No,

Erma. I want it there."

Another person might have accepted that and continued with chitchat or gone on about whatever they were doing. But it was Erma Floyd's business to know why the man wanted his hat on the ground.

"Why, Mr. Jensen? Why would a person want his hat on the ground?" she asked, as if that incongruence had somehow disturbed her world.

And it was a good question, thought the man – one that required the mental agility of which he might no longer be capable. But he tried.

"Eh," he said, stalling for time. "Eh… because it allows perspective."

Erma Floyd seemed stumped by that answer, as most people would have been. Most people, though, would have passed it off as the man's eccentricity or assumed that they themselves were too shallow to understand the meaning of the statement. Erma Floyd was not most people.

"What on earth do you mean by that, Mr. Jensen? I don't understand." Erma Floyd's vocal inflection left no doubt that if she did not understand, the explanation was somehow in error.

The man realized that, if he did not do something soon, Erma Floyd would probe and badger until the man was forced to reveal the truth or come off, as she implied, like a blithering idiot. He did not wish his few remaining friends and relatives to think he was the sort of person who talked to bugs. Besides, the whole process of explanation would take time. The one thing the man did not have was time.

"Perspective, Erma Floyd. You know, the juxtaposition of objects from the viewer that allows a different appreciation of the objects," the man said, holding his ground.

But Erma Floyd was obviously not to be put off. So as she made to respond, the man tried again. "The hat is a small and relatively spherical object which contrasts to the voluptuousness of the female body in full flower viewed from bottom to top." The man leered and winked.

Erma Floyd's eyes gradually opened to full width as the import of the man's statement sank in. "Humph," she said. Then, "Good day, Mr. Jensen." People like Erma Floyd were to know, not to be known. And certainly not to be known in a sexual context.

When Erma Floyd was safely out of sight and no one else was around, the man removed his hat from the bug. The bug flared his wings as if to fly.

"What impressive wings you have, bug, but please don't fly away. I apologize for my rude behavior. However, I was concerned that the large female human would step on you," the man lied.

The bug folded his wings, but remained still.

"It seems that you cannot speak in a language that I understand, but perhaps we can still communicate if you are willing to help me."

The bug didn't move.

The man assumed that meant the bug was willing, so he continued. "Let's try this: I'll ask you questions that can be answered either yes or no. If your answer is yes, do nothing. If your answer is no, move your arm... or whatever that is in front. OK?"

The bug did nothing.

"First question: When beings die, are they reborn as a different living being?"

The bug did nothing.

"Good. Is it true that your good or bad behavior in a prior life determines the form in which you return in your next life?"

The bug did nothing.

"So. If you were good, you come back as a higher form of life, and if you were bad, you come back as a lower form of life. Is that right?"

The bug did nothing.

"When you come back, is it all of your being? I mean, as opposed to just some part of your being in another vessel?"

The bug did nothing.

"Then is it fair to say that you were a very bad something in a former life?"

At first the bug did nothing, then spread his wings.

"Are you saying it's none of my business?"

The bug did nothing.

"When you die, will you become a higher being?"

The bug did nothing.

"Do you remember your former life when you come back as a different being?"

The bug did nothing at first, then seemed to move his front leg.

The man could think of nothing else to ask that might be answerable by the bug. If he had been good, he would be something even greater than a human being and this would take place in the near future. He hoped he had been good enough.

"Thank you, bug. You have eased my mind immeasurably. I wish there was something I could do for you," he said as he made ready to leave. Then, as the meaning of their conversation solidified in his mind, he stepped squarely on the bug and walked away.

"That bug was lying. If a bug can't remember his former life, how would he know anything about being something other than a bug?" he muttered to himself. "Maybe I should ask Erma Floyd. She surely knows more than a bug, and perhaps I can help her along, as well."

NATURE'S WAY

"Goddammit, Carlos. Watch that gun." Harlan Wilks was addressing Carlos Contraras as they made their way along a utilities easement in the predawn hours.

"Sorry, dude," Carlos said, offering no explanation. None was really necessary. It was dark. They weren't very familiar with the area, and a flashlight was out of the question. The good news was the gun wasn't loaded yet. At least, it wasn't supposed to be loaded yet.

"I think we're crazy not having some kind of light." Billy Powers, the third member of the little hunting party, offered his two-cents worth. It didn't really matter what was said, Billy Powers always had something to add. "A feller could break his damn leg wanderin' around up here in the dark."

"Well, Billy." Harlan stopped to catch his breath. "We could wait 'til daybreak and drive over here in your pickup, but the elk might suspect something was up. Ya think?"

Billy resisted the temptation to say "Fuck you, Harlan." Harlan was right and unnecessary talking wouldn't help either.

Harlan, Carlos, and Billy went back past high school. Somewhere in middle school they had found each other, and since then had been inseparable. Sports, girls, but especially hunting – they had always been together, forming a bond so strong that it had lasted into their retirement years. Of course, wives, children, and jobs necessitated some changes, but over the years, they had found a way to meet for one occasion or another. One of those occasions was Saturday, sacred to each. Come hell or high water, Saturday afternoon would find them at the River Run Sports Tavern.

"Heard about this deal," Harlan volunteered over the sounds of TV football.

"I don't want to steal nothin'," Billy responded.

Harlan and Carlos exchanged a look. One of the few

times they had been separated had been when the U.S. Army drafted Billy. Now, as a result of being repeatedly too close to rifle fire, Billy was fast losing his hearing.

"No, Billy. A 'deal', not 'steal.'" Harlan raised his voice several decibels, enunciating each word clearly.

"Oh," said Billy. "So what is it?"

Harlan rearranged his position to put Billy between him and Carlos, so he would now be talking through Billy. "An outfit up the mountain's gonna let a few hunters loose on the elk out of season to thin the herd. I was thinkin' about signin' up. Whadaya think?"

"I don't know, Harlan. Haven't picked up my rifle in quite a few years. Don't know if it still works. Hell, don't know if I still work." Carlos laughed.

"Aw, bullshit, Carlos. You was always a better shot than me and Harlan, and we were better'n anyone I ever saw." Billy thought a minute. "You remember them hunts we used to go on? Boy, did we have some fun. Sittin' around swappin' lies most of the night. Drinkin' a little whiskey. Trackin' most of the day. Draggin' them big fuckers back to camp." He paused. "Guess I could do without the draggin' part."

"He's right," Harlan said. "I'll bet with a little target practice, we'd be just fine. And you know, this might be our last chance to do it." Harlan gave his friends a meaningful look.

"Yeah, I remember. Man, we'd pop them boogers from way off. Almost never miss. Bring back way more meat than we could eat. My family would bug me about when we were goin' out again." Carlos.

"Yeah, we were tough *hombres*. Walk forever. Stay out in any kind of weather to get just one more shot." Harlan.

With that, the three old buckaroos fell into silence mentally reliving hunts past.

"Hell, I'm in," Billy proclaimed.

"I guess me too," Carlos agreed.

As the population of second-home owners had expanded in the mountain valley, some of the predators had been driven out. Grizzly bears, for one, did not live well with human beings. It seemed that grizzlies felt they were the top of the food chain and had little compunction about gobbling up a human now and then. Humans, not being content to live side by side with anything that might eat them, shot the bears with such regularity that the grizzlies that weren't shot left.

So now the elk in the area had no natural predator, and, unlike the grizzlies, they flourished among the second homes and golf courses. The elk-hunting season did not fill the vacuum left by the grizzlies.

At first blush, an elk herd seemed like a nice folksy addition to the big development up in the mountains above the interstate. The golfers and the vacationing homeowners thought it was just real "natural" watching the elk and listening to them bellow in rutting season. What the homeowners did not like was the elk devouring their manicured yards as well as the low-lying shrubs and young trees that made up the surrounding scenic beauty of the neighborhood.

Although that situation might have been tolerable had it remained relatively stable, with no natural predators, the local elk herd continued to increase in number to the point that, even with the buffet offered by the development, the elk were starving in winter. If no action were taken, the herd would eventually denude the high-dollar development and still lose many members to starvation.

The best solution to the problem, the least expensive, and the one endorsed by the forest service, was to unleash a controlled group of professional hunters on the elk herd. It would be a win-win situation. The herd would be thinned, so it could continue to function as nature intended. Maybe the diminished herd would even confine its munching to non-ornamental plants. And the resulting elk meat could be eaten by humans, as opposed to rotting in the forest after the elk had starved. It was also the most humane approach – assuming an elk would rather be shot with a high-powered rifle than starve.

In any case, that's why Harlan, Carlos, and Billy were stumbling around in the dark trying to locate the best vantage point for shooting unsuspecting elk. These men were only concerned with shooting elk. They accepted the justification – if they needed one, after all these years – that it was better to shoot the elk than let them starve.

"It's cold, bro." Carlos, who had now strapped his rifle over his back, blew warm breath into his cupped hands as he spoke. "Where we gonna set up?"

"I can't see nothin'. This place was a lot easier to find yesterday... when it was daylight," Billy whispered.

"I think we just keep walkin' 'til we run outta trail,

and that's the place." Harlan.

"Then you better tell us when that is 'cause I damn sure can't see nothin'." Carlos.

"What if we run outta trail and just wander off a cliff?" Billy, the optimist.

For what seemed like forever, they crept.

"Shit," Harlan cussed, when he ran into a small tree. "I think this is the place. There ain't no more trail."

Almost as if practiced, the three assembled their folding stools, sat, and loaded the rifles. After adjusting one thing and another, they waited, peering into the darkness. There was no moon. No lights from the houses nearby. Even the highway noise that usually permeated the valley was absent. The quiet was such that their ears seemed to ring.

"Man, what time is it?" Carlos whispered to anyone who might know.

"Looks like about six-thirty," Harlan replied in kind.

"We ought to be seein' some light by now," Billy suggested. "Must be overcast, huh?"

"Anybody watch the weather?" Harlan.

"Nothin' special. Partly cloudy to clear. Temperature around thirty." Billy.

"This ain't no 'partly cloudy and thirty.' I'm guessin' low twenties and cloudy. Man, it feels like snow." Carlos.

"Aw, bullshit. Ain't gonna snow in October." Billy.

"Sometimes it does, dude." Carlos.

"If you guys don't quit talkin', it ain't gonna matter if it snows or not." Harlan.

On the way up the mountain, they had laid out the rules of engagement, so to speak. From what they remembered from yesterday's scouting, there was a clearing about fifty yards from where they set up. If they were lucky, and a bunch of the herd showed up at the same time, they'd wait until they were all in the clearing. Then take the animals, left to right, in alphabetical order: Billy, Carlos, then Harlan. The bulls were off limits. They were only authorized to shoot the cows.

At this time of year, there would likely be six to eight cows and a bull somewhere off in the bush. After years of wandering through this wildlife corridor, none of the elk, especially the cows, would be wary. Nobody ever bothered them. Even the local dogs had to be kept on leashes. The phrase "shootin' fish in a barrel" seemed to fit. For guys like Billy, Carlos, and Harlan, there wasn't much sport involved at all.

"Aw, man. Is that rain?" Carlos.

"Could be snow." Billy

"You guys be quiet. It's gettin' light now." Harlan.

As Billy had suggested, it was an overcast dawn. Heavy dull clouds sealed off the sunrise. On the extreme right and down, moving shapes could just be discerned among the low bushes and barren aspen. Now nobody spoke, but it looked like two, maybe three, cows with their heads down grazing were meandering up the ridge into the open. Behind them, two youngsters – also cows.

From out of the brush at the top of the ridge appeared a magnificent bull, head held high sporting an incredible rack. Perhaps a six-hundred pounder.

Wow, all three thought in silent unison, *too bad about the rules*.

It was almost as if the entire ridge had come to life. Dark figures moving slowly, blindly following the lead cows. In the silence, the sound of dragging hooves and munching grass drifted toward the hunters.

Still it was too soon and a bit too dark to shoot. The hunters knew why they were there. They were not new at this.

No hurried shots. Wait. Wait. Only take the sure thing. Nobody wanted to be chasing a wounded elk around in the forest.

It was just then that the wind picked up from the west, and the ridge, which had begun to lighten with the gray dawn, again grew dark. The men glanced at one another but said nothing. Something was happening.

Usually in the mountains, precipitation began slowly and grew, if it did, to a crescendo. But sometimes it didn't. Sometimes it just dumped.

The elk seemed to sense it and held their positions just off the clearing. Then a white curtain fell like it was being shoveled off a roof. Great wet flakes falling in straight-down profusion.

"Shit," whispered Billy. "I can't see nothin'. I can barely see you." He nodded at Harlan. "And you don't look good to eat." Billy chuckled.

"Just be quiet. Maybe it'll pass," Harlan whispered.

And so they sat and waited… and waited. Still it came in white torrents.

"Man," Carlos started.

"Shhhh," cautioned Harlan.

"I got your 'shhhh.' Man, I don't care if they can hear me or not. Look at me. I'm turnin' into a snowman – an old snowman. Man, it's time to put a wrap on this bullshit."

"I'm with you, Carlos," Billy chimed in. "I'm too old for this shit."

As Carlos and Billy made ready to leave, Harlan began to argue. "This stuff could let up, you know? Once upon a time we'd've stayed." *On the other hand, catching a good chill could keep me down for weeks,* Harlan thought even as he made a show of huffing. But then he gave up as well as he realized that, even though they could now sorta see where they were going, the trail had vanished in the snow.

Billy broke the silence on the ride home. "An October dump – what was that all about?"

"Must be global warming." Carlos sniggered.

Harlan added, "Humph. Everything changes."

THE APPEAL

"GODDAMN."

The word had started while Marvin was still in his car, but ended echoing in his head somewhere else. The profane exclamation had been in reaction to the sudden and shocking realization that some asshole in a Hummer had fudged the red light and was accelerating toward Marvin mere yards from his driver-side door.

"Interesting greeting." The man in the white linen suit raised his eyebrows, then shrugged. "But good day to you, as well."

What is this? wondered Marvin. He wasn't exactly frightened, only bewildered. He remembered the Hummer. He didn't remember the crash or any pain. And now he seemed to be in what resembled a white marble hotel lobby. A man resembling Ricardo Montelban stood behind the reception desk peering intently at him. Perhaps he was dreaming of *Fantasy Island.*

"I just look like Ricardo Montelban," the man said, as if Marvin had spoken. Marvin didn't think he had responded. "He no longer needs the image," the man continued, "and I always thought it was rather well done. You're not dreaming and this isn't *Fantasy Island.* You may call me Mr. Peters."

"Well…" Marvin started, then stopped.

"Yep. This is what you people call the 'pearly gates' and I'm the gatekeeper. And to put everything in its place, you're Marvin Thomas Moore, age fifty-nine – until just a few minutes ago. You had a lovely wife Polly and two rather uneventful children, who at age thirty-something are still 'trying to find themselves'."

"You mean I'm…" Marvin couldn't say it.

"Dead?" Mr. Peters helped out, nodding sympathetically. "Yes, I afraid you are. But it wasn't all that bad, now was it? You people spend half your lives worrying about dying, and then suddenly, there it is and that's that. No muss, no fuss. The only people who think it's just awful are the ones who have to clean up the mess you leave behind."

"Well…" Marvin considered the question. "No, I guess it wasn't. I mean, like you say, I was just there and now I'm here." Marvin felt numb. Then a thought occurred to him. "Eh, sorry about the, eh, last word. You know, the first thing I said. I didn't mean anything by it. I was just shocked when that damned, eh, darned – 'darned' is OK, isn't it? – Hummer came barreling at me."

Mr. Peters rolled his eyes. "That's really one of the least of your problems, Marvin. By my calculation, you've uttered at least one obscene or profane or blasphemous word every day since you got out of grade school. That would be well in excess of seventeen thousand small black dings on your account."

"Oh," Marvin said. He did not like the way this was going. "Do you suppose there's been some mistake? I really need to get back to Polly and my practice. Not to mention my idiot kids. Somebody's got to kick 'em in the butt or they'll sleep all day." He paused again. "Did you know we're having a recession down there? Eh, is it *down* there?" Marvin made a gesture of uncertainty with his hands. "If I don't work, they don't eat. And I've got debts out the wazoo. And…"

Mr. Peters raised his palm signifying Marvin should stop. "We don't make mistakes here. *Heaven Can Wait* was a movie. Whatever we do here is, by definition, correct. You see, we make the rules. And it's an *ad hoc* process. No such thing as 'not fair' if we do it. Our actions *are* reality."

Sounds like the government. Must be nice, Marvin thought.

"It isn't nice or not nice. It just *is*," Mr. Peters answered.

Damn, I hate that, Marvin thought. Then, *Oh shit*. Grimacing, he said, "I can't help it. It's just... me."

"I know, and that's a problem," Mr. Peters said, tight-lipped.

Marvin tried not to think.

"But getting back to the business at hand, it says here..." Mr. Peters glanced at what looked like a computer-generated teleprompter. "You died this date when hit by a speeding automobile. No mistake."

Aha, Marvin thought. *It wasn't an automobile. Technically it was a truck.*

"No 'Aha', Marvin. We don't deal in technicalities, and besides that, 'automobile' is a generic term. It covers Hummers."

"Why'd you have to check?" Marvin said out loud. Didn't matter anyway.

"Even if we don't make mistakes, we do keep records – even though we don't forget, either." Mr. Peters seemed a bit snippy.

Marvin started to think something, but willed himself not to. "Mr. Peters, I can't be dead. I had eighteen years left. At least, that's the average. I could have had more. I love my wife and I don't want to leave her yet, and my partners'll screw me if I'm not there to make sure they don't." Marvin exuded distress.

"I'm really sorry, Marvin, but there is nothing I can do. You were supposed to die. You did die. And here you are. If I made an exception for you, in a case like this, I'd almost literally have to do it for everybody. Besides that, I'm really not the one in charge here. There's… you know… Him."

"Can I talk to Him?" Marvin shot back.

"You never did before," Mr. Peters answered even quicker.

"You mean there's some kind of statute of limitations? Because I didn't before, I can't do it now?" Marvin had not been the firm's litigation specialist for nothing. He could think on his feet – if that was a fair description under these circumstances.

"We don't have statutes, and if we did, we wouldn't have limitations. We do have rules, though. And one of those rules is that this is my call." Pause. "Unless, of course, He decides it isn't. Which brings me to our next order of business."

Marvin, of course, couldn't be sure what the next order of business was, but if all the jokes he'd ever heard were right, this is when he got the old "thumbs up, thumbs down" routine.

"Will it help if I cower?" Marvin said.

"Don't be a smartass," Mr. Peters answered. "That definitely won't help."

Mr. Peters gestured with his right hand, and to the accompaniment of a harp, one of those teleprompter things appeared to his right. He gestured with his left hand, and a similar phenomenon occurred on his left, only with the sound of a chord played on the bass end of a piano.

"Let me guess," said Marvin. "These are high-tech representations of my good and bad deeds in life."

"There you go again," said Mr. Peters, as the list on

the left almost imperceptibly lengthened.

"I apologize. Force of habit," said Marvin. "But it doesn't seem fair to add stuff on my bad list after I'm already dead. Isn't that kind of like adding in unadjudicated extraneous offenses in a trial?"

Mr. Peters thought a moment. The length of the list on the left remained the same. "There is no such thing as 'unadjudicated' here. If it happens, it's judged. So let's see what we've got. Looks like you were a pretty good person in high school. Didn't cheat, hurt people, or tear things up. Studied hard. Graduated high in your class. Didn't have sex with your steady girl, Betty Sue Graham. Considering you were a teenager, you were a pretty good son to your parents. Then you went to college and..."

"Eh, hey, Mr. Peters, what about before high school? I was a really good kid before high school. What about that?"

"Doesn't count. It's like a juvenile record." He translated for Marvin's benefit. "Before a certain age, we figure you don't know enough to be really bad. You simply do stuff that kids do." Mr. Peters focused in thought for a moment. "That seems to be changing a bit now for some reason – probably TV or video games – but it still doesn't apply to you. Your list starts at high school." He gave Marvin a meaningful look. "As I was saying, then you went to college and your behavior went straight to hell. Excuse the pun." Mr. Peters allowed himself a chuckle.

Marvin did not share the heavenly humor.

"Says here you joined a fraternity and began being mean to girls who weren't considered attractive. I see you even participated in a 'pig party.' Hmm. Not good, Marvin."

Marvin was silent. He had no real excuse.

"I know you want to say that it was because you were influenced by others."

Marvin nodded hopefully.

"And that's probably true, but it remains that you callously and without justification hurt other people."

"I am truly sorry," said Marvin, and he really was.

"At this point, 'sorry' won't cut it. This one stays on the list."

Marvin swallowed hard.

"On the other hand, you did do very well academically without cheating. That's definitely a plus. And once you rescued a lost puppy from a storm sewer. Not a major deal, but it might offset some of your foul language. And, ah yes, this is good. In your senior year you tutored some disadvantaged kids. But then, that was so you could get close to the program director, Loretta Swank... and you did get close to her."

"Why is that bad? It sounds like a win-win to me. The kids got some help. I made Loretta happy. No harm, no foul. I think that oughta be a double plus."

"Does the word fornication ring a bell, Marvin?"

"Well sure. But the 'Big Ten' doesn't say anything about fornication and this wasn't my neighbor's wife. This was just two consenting adults enjoying each other. Surely that can't be wrong." Marvin made the point and stopped.

"Didn't read much Bible, eh Marvin? Trust me. That one goes in the negative column under one of the Seven Deadlies."

Marvin's shoulders drooped.

"Well, let's see. You got into law school and did well there, too, graduating in the top ten percent of your class. Your strong suit seems to have been in the intellectual area. Too bad you couldn't keep it in your pants and just study." Mr. Peters gave Marvin a snide glance. "Then started your own law firm. Made money. Made more money. Got married.

Had kids. Yada. Yada. Yada."

"'Yada. Yada. Yada.'" Marvin huffed. "You talk like that was nothing. It was hard work."

"Relax, Marvin. You get credit. It's just nothing, you know, spectacular. Lots of people do it and don't make a lot of money."

"What about charity?" Marvin asked.

"I see. And that's a big plus. Not exactly a tithe, but better than most people. And the tax deduction didn't hurt either."

Marvin was bumfuzzled. "That's the way it works down there. You don't give money away for nothing."

Mr. Peters stopped his busywork and regarded Marvin thoughtfully. "You know, Marvin, that's why you're not getting full credit, so to speak. Charity is something done from the heart to help out with the human condition. Of course, it's not bad that everybody seems to win with charity balls and tax deductible gifts, but it's not quite… 'selfless' – I guess is the word – not really a pure act of love."

You do what you can, Marvin thought out of habit.

"That's true, and you get what's coming to you, as well." Mr. Peters countered.

Marvin threw up his hands in futility.

"But you were doing OK until you had a one-night stand with your secretary. Pretty girl, though." Mr. Peters pursed his lips.

"I had too much to drink that night. And it never happened again," Marvin protested.

"If that's an excuse, it won't wash. It's like saying 'I did a bad thing because I did a bad thing.' You had a little problem with booze, didn't you, Marvin?" He continued studying both lists. "Uh oh. Looks like you took some money from the partnership fund that you weren't entitled to. Correct me if I'm wrong, but I think that's covered under Number Three of His direct Commandments. What's that all about?"

"It wasn't really stealing. I was temporarily short of funds. It was more of a loan. I just never got around to paying it back. It's more like a bad debt," Marvin explained.

"Oh. The money wasn't yours. You took it. And you never paid it back. How is that not in direct violation of 'Thou Shall Not Steal'?" For a saintly guy, Mr. Peters had a large sarcastic streak.

"If you take something and intend to give it back, but

don't, it's a bad debt. If you take something never intending to give it back, and you don't, it's theft. You see, it all has to do with when the intent to keep the thing was formed." Marvin was pleased with his explanation.

"And if you didn't intend not to give it back, you get to keep it if you later decided not to give it back?" Mr. Peters looked confused.

"No. You have to give it back either way, if you've still got it. But in one case, it's a criminal matter and the other it's a civil matter. Down there, we think of criminal as evil, but civil is more like bad judgment or a mistake."

"I don't think we recognize that distinction up here, but I do understand why people tend to distrust lawyers. That stays on the bad list. And let's see," said Mr. Peters, getting back to business. "You never went to a church service."

"I coached Little League."

"You never observed the Holy Days."

"I helped a Boy Scout across the street once and kept a real nice yard."

"OK. We'll call that a wash, but here's something a bit more damning. Pun intended." Mr. Peters smiled. "Our records indicate that you took a bribe from opposing counsel to lose a big oil and gas case."

That stopped Marvin's spirited self-defense cold. It was true. He had no good excuse. But being a lawyer, he tried anyway. "Both sides had so much money they didn't know what to do with it. My client may have been legally right on this one, but he'd been legally wrong on lots more stuff. He just hadn't been caught."

"So... what? You were actually an avenging angel?" Mr. Peters looked skeptical.

"Yeah. Pretty much," Marvin replied.

"Wrong move, Marvin. Contrition was the ticket. And that's about it, except..." Mr. Peters let that hang. "Let's see. Dadadada. Oh, here it is. You represented a child molester once. Hmm." Mr. Peters looked very grave.

"Mr. Peters!?! That was my job. Every person charged with a crime is entitled to zealous representation by counsel." Marvin was incensed.

"How about, say, Judas Escariot? Hmm?" Mr. Peters projected a lupine glare.

"Well..." *This isn't fair*, thought Marvin.

"I've already explained about *fair*, Marvin."

"Look, Mr. Peters. That's a multifarious question.

Damned if I do, damned if I don't." Marvin immediately realized what he'd just said and grimaced.

Mr. Peters smiled.

"I mean it's like asking if you still beat your wife. Whatever you say, you lose."

Mr. Peters adopted an air of strained patience. "Marvin, I know you haven't been inside, but if you had been, you'd notice a real poverty of lawyers." He paused. "Know why?"

Marvin knew why. "OK. I'll answer the question. Yes. Judas would have gotten a lawyer in the United States."

"Yes, I understand that. But do you think Judas Escariot should have legal representation? That's the question."

"Honestly…" Marvin began.

"That might be a good idea," Mr. Peters interrupted.

"Sorry. Just a stutter-step. It depends on where we're talking about."

"Is this like the definition of 'is'?" Mr. Peters interrupted again, rolling his eyes.

"No. Stay with me here," Marvin implored. "You see, in the world we can't know everything. And sometimes accusations by the government are wrong. When it's the government against the individual, the little guy doesn't really have a chance. So to help find the truth, the little guy needs some help. So yeah, on earth Judas needs a lawyer." Marvin paused. "Now if you're up here, you guys already know the truth. Or put another way, the 'government' always knows the truth. So no, here Judas doesn't get a lawyer."

"Hmm. Not bad, Marvin. It won't win the day, but it'll help."

That didn't compute for Marvin. *How could it help but not win? Maybe we're talking "counts" like in federal court.*

"Kind of like that," Mr. Peters answered. "This'll just take a minute. Be patient." Mr. Peters proceeded to make notes. Scratch this. Add that. Then he stopped and looked gravely at Marvin. "Sorry, Marvin. You lose. It's back to earth for you."

Marvin slumped, a defeated warrior. Then "Whadaya mean 'I lose?' I get to go back. I win." Marvin beamed.

"Marvin." Mr. Peters displayed a kind of Mona Lisa smile. "I said you get to go back to earth. I didn't say what you get to go back to earth as."

WALTER MITTY RIDES AGAIN

(A tribute to James Thurber)

"That's him," Commander Wellington Mithers muttered, as his battle-tested eyes honed to the swarthy slinking figure of Akmed Al-Kaball. "Gotcha."

Al-Kaball was oblivious to the presence of The Company's ace antiterrorist hunter. That was because Wally, as his friends knew Commander Mithers, sat slouched against a huge ceramic vase holding an artificial palm tree bedecked with green and red seasonal lights. Who would suspect this grubby unshaven street person, with a sign saying "Help Me Get Home for Christmas" tilted against a timeworn hat that doubled as a collection plate, was in fact a government super-snoop? Even Al-Kaball, known as "The Crow" for his skill at evading capture, had his limitations.

Many had tried to thwart the evil Al-Kaball and ended up empty-handed or dead. Many were the victims of this crazed and fanatical mass murderer. And if the intel was correct, Al-Kaball was at this very time on such a homicidal mission.

To his credit, Wally thought, Al-Kaball blended with the meandering crowds of innocent Christmas shoppers. No one would suspect a maintenance man pushing a trash barrel to be anything other than part of the faceless human infrastructure of a big-city mall. No one could know that inside that grease-spattered trash receptacle he lazily directed along the walkway was a plylytherium modular explosive with enough destructive force to level an entire city block. In a matter of minutes the happy holiday picture would be converted to a gore-strewn scene from Dante.

Fortunately, the ol' boys at The Farm had gotten wind, by way of a deep-cover mole, that this day would be Al-Kaball's master stroke. They had mobilized perhaps the one man on the planet who could avert disaster: Commander Wellington Mithers, or Wally, as his friends knew him.

Tucked inside the tattered right sleeve of Wally's faded tweed coat was a Colkatravnik GG77 mini-sniper rifle. The Colka was designed for easy concealment and loaded with hollow-point 22.20 high-velocity armor-piercing ammunition. Accurate to thirty yards, the Colka had the knock-down power of the terrorists' weapon *de jour*, the Kalashnikov AK 47. Its only drawback was that it only held one shell. But one shell was all an Olympic-class marksman like Wally would need.

Moving with the stealth of a Gaboon viper, Al-Kaball veered from the line of stores in the direction of the Meet Santa Claus House where excited children waited their turn to share their Christmas desires and fantasies with Old St. Nick himself. A chill ran down the spine of Commander Mithers. *The fiend*, he thought.

As Wally calculated, he had maybe fifty paces to take out the terrorist before he slithered into killing range of Santa's house. *An easy shot*, thought Wally as he slid the Colka from his sleeve and sighted down the small barrel. Tracking the killer through the sight, careful to lead just the right distance, he whispered "Gently, gently" as he slowly applied pressure to the trigger.

But wait. What's this? A group of nuns moved to block

Wally's target line.

"Wally! Why are you pointing that pencil at the maintenance man?" It was Wally's wife Estella, who wore a long black coat. "Come on. Let's go. They didn't have anything that would fit. Let's try Morganstern's."

Wally dutifully shook himself into a standing position and waddled off alongside Estella down the walkway toward yet another department store.

Wally hated malls. In fact, Wally hated shopping, and since malls were just a super-concentrated form of hyper-shopping, he hated shopping in malls more than anything. Why he would subject himself to this kind of misery was a mystery. However, he supposed it had something to do with relativity. That is, going to a shopping mall with Estella was better than sitting home by himself watching CNN. Besides, if he survived the experience, they were already dressed for an occasion. So a nice dinner on the way home would be fun.

Nevertheless, accompanying Estella to a mall was an ordeal. Almost all the stores either catered to women or teen-agers or teenaged women. Nothing for a guy to do. He had tried going into the stores with Estella, but that was worse than doing nothing outside the stores. Sitting in a store while a bunch of women tried on clothes made him feel like on old pervert.

Why, he wondered, *are there no places for men in malls? A nice sports bar or a gun shop would make a trip to the mall a much more satisfying event.* It seemed like a win-win-win-win situation. The men's places would make money and the men would be happier with something to do. The women would get to shop longer, so they would be happier and the women's stores would make even more money.

But nobody had asked Wally, and as he looked around, he could see only older men – sitting like statues or captives or statues of captives on the uncomfortable benches in the middle of the walkways outside the stores. There were no young men sitting there. He guessed that the younger men had things to do other than escort their women to malls. The old guys sitting on the benches were clearly not as numerous as the hordes of women shopping. So he assumed that even many older men found something else to do. Wally wondered what that might be. If it was watching television or babysitting grandkids, that wasn't better to Wally's way of thinking. Perhaps they were dead and most of the older women shoppers were widows. *Hmm*, Wally thought.

"Want to come with?" Estella said, as they approached Morganstern's.

Wally frowned. "Come with what? And no, I don't want to come in."

Captain Waldroux Mitterand – face blackened, clad in black, his trusty throwing dagger taped to his inner thigh – belly-crawled in the shadow of the wall. Captain Waldroux Mitterand, Wally to his friends, was a Navy Seal who had been called out of retirement solely for this mission. Many men were available, but none with the skill and cunning of Captain Mitterand, a French-American veteran of the Cold War. The top brass had determined that Wally, and only Wally, could accomplish this mission with any hope of survival. Even then, the chance of Wally coming out alive was miniscule. But he liked those odds.

"Why gamble if the stakes aren't high?" Wally was fond of saying.

It had been decades, and many other wars, since the War to End All Wars had ended. Many gallant soldiers who did not come back had been presumed killed in action. Loved ones had reluctantly adjusted and life had gone on for the living.

Then just recently, during a routine camping trip, a troop of Boy Scouts had stumbled upon a top secret Nazi interment camp in the heart of Mississippi.

Having something get completely lost in the backwoods of Mississippi wasn't entirely unusual or surprising. However, something of this magnitude stretched the boundaries of "just plain damn weird." First, the size of the camp was incredible. From the outside, it appeared cruciform in shape, camouflaged with kudzu, and about the size of an inner-city high school. Second, the whole structure was surrounded by what appeared to be oddly labeled and lighted landing strips patrolled by marked security vehicles.

Wisely, the Boy Scouts had left quietly the same way they came. When they reported their discovery to the authorities, the authorities – a local sheriff named Virgil – had correctly assumed that anything that strange had to have something to do with the federal government. In almost no time at all, after Virgil reported the discovery to the FBI, the Boy Scouts and Virgil were "invited" to be the extended guests of a military group so secret, it had no Greek-letter designation or code name.

Further recognizance proved almost fruitless. Four Special Forces covert ops were sent in, and all four vanished without a trace. However, before vanishing, one of the men managed to get inside and radio that he thought the whole place was a POW camp. The graybeards at the Pentagon concluded that the radio man was probably on drugs, but if he wasn't, nuking the thing would be out of the question. It was then that the name Captain Waldroux Mitterand, "Wally" to his friends, was mentioned.

In the dead of night in the dark of the moon, Wally had parachuted in from a glider. For a man of Wally's skills, bypassing the security of the perimeter was child's play. Removing a conveniently located and sized air conditioning vent cover, he made his way silently through the duct system of the complex.

It was from this vantage point that Wally discovered the final and most bizarre elements of the complex. It was of course, as everyone had guessed, a POW camp. What made it beyond peculiar were two things. First, the guards were aging Amazon women. With a little sneakin' and peekin', Wally quickly learned that these Amazon women were Germans whose husbands had given it up for the Axis powers. Second, the prisoners were Allied troops kept chained in the center of walkways between the guards' quarters. They were apparently sex slaves held for the perverse gratification of the Amazons.

It was instantly clear to Wally that he would have to single-handedly undertake an immediate rescue. *These guys are old. How much more can they take?*

Killing the power with plastic explosives, Wally now slithered along the wall of the guards' quarters toward the imprisoned warriors. It was his plan to pick the lock securing their chains with his trusty throwing dagger, then lead them through the darkened walkways to freedom.

Then Wally began to worry. *After so long in captivity and subjugation, can they still communicate in English? Do they still have the will to survive? What if they resist escaping?*

He had to chance it. Slowly he crept into position. Gently lifting the heavy iron lock to avoid a telltale clank that would bring the guards, Wally inserted the metal tip of his dagger into the keyhole. He could feel the little tumblers begin to fall into place. In just seconds, it would be open and they would be free.

Suddenly, blazing lights illuminated the area. *Drat*, he

thought, *I forgot about the auxiliary power system.* A huge dark shadow crossed from above.

"Wally, what are you doing crawling under that man's bench?" Estella had finished her foray into Morganstern's.

"I dropped my pencil. I was just getting it." Wally slipped the pencil from his vest pocket and displayed it to Estella. "No luck?" he changed the topic.

"Oh, they had a couple of things, but…" Estella made a futile gesture. "Can you stand one more place?" She paused. "Then we can go to dinner and have a cocktail."

Making a great show of abused innocence, Wally walked with Estella in the direction of a new chain store in the mall, Cold Duck Stream. And it wasn't all show. During the time Estella had spent in the stores, Wally had sat, paced, and done a little crawling on the hard marble surface that was the mall. All of him, but especially his feet, hurt. His former bouncy waddle had degenerated into a struggling meander.

Why, he wondered, *did the mall floor have to be so hard? Wouldn't it make more sense to use carpet? Maybe carpet over wood? That way people wouldn't get so tired. Then they wouldn't leave so soon. But nobody asked me.*

Wally wasn't sure if he could make it to Cold Duck Stream, but in fairly short order, there they were.

"I'll be quick," said Estella.

"Bullshit," muttered Wally under his breath.

"Pardon?" said Estella.

"Nothing," answered Wally, as he felt his spine collapse.

Wing Commander Waldo O'Mittery stood silently peering from the barred window of his cell. It was just as well that it was too dark to see much. In a matter of hours, the sun would rise and he would meet his fate. That would be soon enough to see the surroundings.

Wing Commander O'Mittery, Wally to his friends, couldn't really despair and bemoan his fate. He had asked for the assignment. He recalled the words of Prime Minister Churchill to the assembled elite of the elite.

"Gentlemen, your country needs your help now more than ever before. The Nazi is destroying our lives, our cities, our very culture, nightly with his buzz bombs and V1 rockets. If this tiny island nation is to survive, we must strike at the heart of fascism. We must cleave the head so the body will die. We must attack Berlin with our guns, our hearts, our souls, with all we are and ever hope to be. We must prevail. This mission your country asks of you is beyond dangerous. Many, perhaps most, of you will not return. But know this: because of your gallant action, our country, our wives, our children, our world will survive to a new and better day. You are the elite of the elite, and under Wing Commander O'Mittery, you will do what must be done for King and country. Now make us proud, lads."

After that, the Prime Minister seemed to disappear in a cloud of cigar smoke and all the flyboys began preparations in earnest to hurl themselves into the teeth of the enemy.

The night had been dark and overcast – perfect for an air attack. The channel was quiet. The whole thing had an aura of unreality. Maybe they would fly in, drop their payload, and return home safe. Piece of cake.

Then Lady Luck poked them right in the eye with the fickle finger of fate. Over Berlin, the clouds dissipated, and the Gerries opened up with everything they had. It seemed that someone couldn't keep a secret. The Germans were ready for them.

Flak to the left. Flak to the right. "I'm hit. I'm hit."

Luftwaffe everywhere. It was time to turn around. Somehow King and country were getting lost in the shuffle.

"Did we hit the target?" Wally radioed. "I repeat. Can anyone confirm a kill?"

No answer. Then a Scottish accent: "Commander, we're all shot to hell. The planes won't take no more."

Wally knew these men weren't cowards. They were just beaten. There was only one thing to do.

"Disengage. I repeat. Disengage." Wally gave the command. But as the wing headed west and home, Wally pulled hard on the stick, taking his plane out of formation and back to the battle. He had seen the ammo depot and he wasn't going home without it.

Flying low, the ack-ack guns were miscalibrated for his altitude. They were missing badly above him. The Luftwaffe was busy chasing what was left of his command. His path was clear.

Sighting the ammo plant, he pushed the stick forward using his aircraft as a guided missile. With seconds to spare, he ejected and popped his chute. It was a glorious sight when the whole plant exploded as he floated to the ground.

Unfortunately for Wally, with the light from all the

explosions, the enemy had no trouble seeing exactly where he was going to land and they were right there waiting when he touched down – not so gently.

Now Wally could see the dawn breaking and he knew it wouldn't be long. It was a little odd that the gallows was so far from the prison. Perhaps they would drive him over. On the other hand, he really wasn't in much of a hurry.

With a clank at his cell door, the guards entered and briskly escorted Wally out of his cell and down a long series of steps. Not that it mattered much at a time like this, but somewhere along the way, he had lost his boots. He was now barefooted, and as they finally left the prison building, he began to feel shooting pain in his feet and knees. With still over a hundred yards to the gallows, each step became agony. He was not sure he could even get there. It would be really embarrassing to have to be carried to one's own execution.

But, stiff upper lip and all, Wally continued step after excruciatingly painful step. *Just put one foot in front of the other*, he thought to himself. *I can make it.* "Make them proud of you." The words rang in his ears, but the pain, the terrible pain, was too much. Within yards of the gallows, he dropped to his knees and began to crawl, telling himself over and over, *I can do this. I can do this.* At last he was there, standing with the noose around his neck.

"Wing Commander, are there any last words?" said the grim executioner in heavily accented English.

"I have but one thing to say..." Wally began.

"I know exactly what you're going to say. 'Can we go to dinner now?' And yes. I'm beat." It was Estella. It was blessedly time for a drink.

"Sorry you didn't find anything," Wally said over a double martini at the restaurant.

"Oh, I'll find something sooner or later. I just hate to spend all day for nothing." Estella paused in thought. "But I guess it was harder for you – spending all day doing nothing but waiting for me." She smiled and touched his hand.

"Actually, ma darlin' girl, it was pretty exciting," Wally said with a bit of a brogue.

AFTERLIFE

It doesn't look much different than it did ten years ago. But then, the park probably hasn't changed much since the WPA and the National Park Service started building trails and such.

For me, it isn't the discrete passage of time. It's more the shift from one lifetime to another. Much like the experience of going back to your old high school or the house you were born in. The change isn't external. Something within is so radically different that whatever is on the outside must be different.

On a sunny day in early October, Acadia's beauty defies my prosaic powers. The brilliant foliage seems to reflect all the colors of nature in a comfortable satisfying warmth, while the occasional breeze reminds the off-season tourist that winter will not allow this mellow state for long. Blend the craggy timeworn stone cliffs and the occasional glimpse of the battering waves of the stormy Atlantic Ocean, and there's no place to compare for those who worship the out-of-doors. The delusion that God is in his heaven and all's right with the world is inescapable. And maybe that's the truth. Who knows what God thinks about?

As I stare at the black lettering on the gaudy yellow sign at the foot of The Precipice trail, it could have been ten years ago: "CAUTION! EXPOSED FACES AND IRON RUNGS. PEOPLE HAVE DIED HERE." The last part added like the "this means you" on the no-parking sign.

But ten years ago, I wasn't alone. Then it was Jane and I who gave passing notice to the warning. But unlike to-day, it was just a thing of interest – almost amusing, nothing that might affect us.

"Do you think we should turn back?" Jane with the mischievous laughing eyes.

"Only if you're ready to cry 'wuss.'" Me with our little game of dare. We both understood that if either of us had real reservations or grew tired of our adventures, there would be no ridicule. The overstatement made it funny.

Then the serious business of climbing. The sign had not exaggerated to scare off the rookies. Iron rungs, hand over hand. Narrow ledges snaking up weathered faces exposed to nothing but a view. Not a trail for the faint of heart or vertically challenged.

In the lead, I shouted over my shoulder, "How're we doin'?"

"Right behind..." Jane's voice started normal and breathless, elevating to something like a shriek.

Turning – and many times I've wished I had not been so quick – I saw the face of my beloved caught in an expression of surprise and terror. Then her quick look of resignation and apology directly into my eyes.

There was no other sound as the person who was my life descended almost in slow motion to a final, barely audible, thump.

Everybody in situations like this always says "the rest was a blur." What else can you say? It was a blur. The pell-mell race down the trail we had just ascended. The alternating emotions from denial to heart-crushing pain to unrealistic hope of survival. The body who was, not ten minutes ago, the center of my existence, now... what? A mangled rag doll, a lifeless thing. The pain. Oh, God, the pain. The disbelief. The shock.

Sometime later people arrived. I didn't know who or why. Now I'd guess they were park rescue workers. The urgent questions. The blankets.

More time elapsed. These strangers decided it was I who needed to go to the hospital. Me? Why me? I was just fine. Or maybe not. I couldn't seem to stop the tears and... howling. Yes, howling. I don't know why. I'd always thought that people who keened were emotional imbeciles. But there it was: howling.

Medical people must be trained in such things. Gentle support while gauging my level of cognition. Administering drugs.

Finally somebody took me back to the motel where I slept, mercifully medicated.

Awaking as if slapped, I was a little surprised to see my son. Not really, I guess. If anyone was going to do anything, it would be him. There wasn't anybody else. Personally I was up for more meds and blissful dreamless nothingness.

He must have understood and honored my wishes, for my next recollection was being helped to dress. I want to say that it was embarrassing, but he was almost forty years old and I had done the same for him once upon a time.

The blur began to fade, interspersed with assaults of brutal reality. The plane ride was the worst. The flight attendants were nice enough and my son was attentive. I wasn't much interested in either. Certainly I didn't wish to chat or explain. My only wish was to stare out the porthole and be left alone to... feel really rotten, I suppose.

How could it possibly be that my life mate wasn't making this trip with me? I don't want to beat a dead horse, so to speak, but I might as well have left my two legs and an arm in Bar Harbor. This cosmic incongruity occasionally swapped places with sweet memory – and some not sweet at all.

The first time I ever saw Jane. The first kiss. The physical intimacy. Stroboscopic scenes from our life. The fall. The second-guessing. *What if she had gone up first? What if it was my question that caused her to lose balance? Why didn't we go to Kansas instead of Maine?*

Then there was the memorial service with the quiet

condolences. Jesus! The condolences. How was I ever going to get through this with all of these sad people accosting me?

Fortunately, we had made a pact: whoever died first would make sure the other one was cremated. I don't think I could have watched a casket lowered into the ground with Jane in it – even if it wasn't really Jane.

And then everyone went home but me. Home was where Jane was and Jane wasn't around anymore.

After thirty-odd years of virtual spiritual unity with another person, I was sixty-something and by myself. I could follow Jane or start something new. And frankly, option one was a lot more appealing than option two.

Spinning positive, I elected to courageously carry on with life. Spinning negative, I was chicken. I mean, have you ever thought about suicide? One little slip and, instead of being blissfully dead, you're a vegetable kept alive by machines or worse.

Besides that, I was kind of curious about what life might be like without my other half. Don't misunderstand. At sixty-something, I'm not talking about wild women and song. But our relationship was one of shared perception. Maybe we just saw things the same way. Maybe without the influence of the other, we would have seen things a little differently.

Believe me, I didn't want to experience anything without Jane. I figured I would just hate it. But what could it hurt to give it a little time and see. If it didn't work out, there was always option one.

But before we get back to the yellow sign in Acadia National Park, I want to tell you how it went – how things were in the life after Jane. Then you'll know if I'm fixin' to follow Jane, looking for closure, or just going out for a hike.

At its very best, it was confusing – at worst, it was horrible. I mean, what does a single old guy do?

I did a lot of sitting and thinking... and drinking at first. It was depression, I suppose, if you want to intellectualize it, but I didn't have the energy or desire to do anything. I guess the good news was I lost some weight. I had always been heavy, not fat, but overweight. Life before had been a perpetual struggle with the scales. Now one of the things I didn't want to do was eat. I ate only when I got too hungry to do otherwise, and it was a bunch of whatever was around the house – cans of stuff that had been in the pantry for who-knows-how-long, food left over from the wake.

As far as I could see, the rest of my life would be this way. It was at this time that I came closest to taking that long last drive in a closed garage. Hell, why not? Anything was better than more canned asparagus.

But then one day my son dropped by. He said he was having a few friends over and wanted me to come. I immediately declined.

"No, son. I just don't think… I…" I began.

"You don't think what? You don't have time?" He cut me off. "As near as I can tell, you don't have anything but time. Unless you need lots of time to wallow in self-pity. Heck, why don't you have a real party and eat your gun?" He had been reading too many cop books. "Dad," he said, beginning to tear. "I still need you."

I guess that did it. He could have said a lot of things that would have counted for nothing in my state, but the fact that he still needed me stirred something deep down, almost primal. If someone, especially my boy, thought I was still necessary, that was enough to pass the tipping point. I would give it a whirl. I went to the party.

The group consisted of my son and daughter-in-law, my son's best friend since grade school and his wife, and a lone woman, about my age. Even without being some kind of shrink, this seemed pretty obvious, but I girded myself to smile and be polite.

Turns out, the lady wasn't interested in hooking-up, as they say now. She was a nice widow who invited me to a group she belonged to. It was a fairly small bunch whose sole purpose was readjusting to living without a spouse or significant other.

"I'd love to come," I said, lying through my smile. I think that's what Jane would have said, but she would have actually gone. I had no intention of going. I was gloomy enough without being around a bunch of other gloomy people.

Fortunately, I suppose, my son had been listening. At the appointed day and time, he showed up at my house to drive me – just in case I refused to drive myself.

I had never needed groups of people. Jane and I had always been plenty. So I had never experienced the power of groups. These people weren't gloomy. Oh sure, there was an occasional sniffle when talking about their lost love, but basically they were trying to find some way to carry on some sort of meaningful life. They were a lot like me. And the main thing was they seemed to genuinely want me to find something worth living for. I guess that's what the psychobabblers mean by "support group." Whatever you call it, it was one of the best feelings I had had since Jane died.

After for-almost-ever, I began to enjoy life a little. Although I felt guilty about it, I was kind of attracted to a woman I met at the grocery store and decided to ask her out. That was funny. At least it would have been, I think, to an observer. It wasn't funny to me. It had been thirty years since I had thought much about any woman except Jane, and forty years since I had worried about asking one out. I actually experienced date-calling anxiety – just like a teenager.

If you're curious, the date worked out just fine. Intimacy with a woman was another story. That took a really long time. But gradually, gradually I began to re-engage with life: joined clubs, dated women, did volunteer work, began to exercise, and, unfortunately, gained weight. And forgot all about Jane?

No. Not even close. Not ever. The bond was too strong to ever break, even if I wanted to. I have a few female friends, but I could never have another soul mate. But I'm doing OK. Life is good.

In a way, I'm lucky. Although Jane left me way too soon, while she lived we had something only the very few and the very fortunate ever have in this world.

So to answer the question I posed earlier, I'm just going for a hike. It's nice here in autumn. After the brash green exuberance of spring, the lazy lushness of summer, the leaves are turning the regal brilliance of reds and golds. Soon they will brown and give themselves to the stark white of winter – the grand design. I can almost feel Jane's presence.

THINGS CHANGE

Randle Grubbs is my name and there are many things in this modern world that I don't understand, but one of my primary areas of ignorance is electronics. The internet, computers, TV remotes – you name it, if it's electronic, I don't understand how it works. I can't even use all the bells and whistles on my car. So I've given up trying.

However, to avoid being left even deeper in the dust of history, I've devised a system to cope. The system is simple; otherwise I wouldn't understand it. Fundamentally, my approach is to find one thing, or button, or way to make something do what I want it to do. After that, I do not vary anything I do to make whatever it is work.

"Never push a new button" is my rule. I recognize

that if I do push a new button, the whole system will go down and I may never be able to get it working again. This is something that has happened repeatedly with accidental touching of TV remotes. Right at the very best part of the movie, I reach for my beer, bump something on the remote, and blip. That's the end of it.

Fortunately, I have a forty-year-old daughter, Gina, who can make anything work. It's almost mystical, as if she were born with this sixth sense. I guess that's common with her generation, but that's not the point. The point is Gina managed to educate me on the fundamentals of using a computer well enough to teach me about the wonders of e-mail. To me, this was a whole new world. It now baffles me that some of my friends don't or can't use e-mail. How can they communicate with the rest of the world?

I suppose the flip side of internet fascination is that I spend too much time on it – time better spent on any number of things, reading being the most prominent. But, getting back to the point, that's what I was doing when the little icon signaled that I had a message.

The message was from somebody or something called "Billywire." Although it sounded suspect and I knew it could be a virus that would eat my whole computer, I opened it.

"If this is the same Randy Grubbs who graduated from Woodrow Wilson in '61, I'd love to hear from you. If it's not you, hit 'delete.' Bill Hamilton."

Well, I'll be darned, I thought. *Bill Hamilton*. Of all the people who might have popped up into my life, Bill Hamilton was not even on my list of possibles. We had gone from first grade through high school together – been best friends through most of that time. Toward the end of high school our fancies had turned radically to the opposite sex, and we weren't so tight anymore. After high school, Bill went off to State and I went to the University. From that point, our paths continued to diverge, I guess. I don't think I've seen him since – almost fifty years.

Of course, I immediately responded with the obvious questions. In reply, Bill explained that he had graduated with a business degree from State and went to work with a large insurance company. Met a girl, married, had two kids, and about the time he retired, his wife decided she wanted a divorce. He didn't go into details. Now he was sorry he'd retired, but he'd relocated to Texas and started a new career as a consultant. He said he'd been dating, but nothing terribly serious, and he was reasonably happy. He didn't mention his kids or grandkids. I wondered what that meant.

I told him that my life had been similar to his, except I had set up shop as a psychologist. I had married a girl I met in college, had three kids, two of whom had now produced grandkids. My wife, unfortunately, had died a few years ago. I was still working, but not in private practice anymore. I taught part-time at the local junior college. Like Bill, I too had dated a bit, and with teaching, my family, and the women I'd met, I enjoyed a pretty good life.

Bill sent me a grainy picture of himself standing in front of a ranch-style house with cactus in the garden. As near as I could tell, his hair was mostly gone and he had put on a few pounds, but he looked tan and healthy. I did not send a picture because Gina had not taught me the mysteries of scanning. But I told him my hair was mostly gray and thinning.

After agreeing that modern technology was impossible, that there were no good TV programs anymore, and that old Mr. Titus, the principal at Woodrow Wilson, had been a jerk, Bill suggested that we get together. Having experienced the wicked ways of the world and wondering if we really had anything in common after all these years, I might have been reticent. However, he explained that old Woodrow Wilson was having a fiftieth class reunion the following month. It seemed to be a good place to meet. Obviously, the reunion would be in Springfield where we had grown up. Although not exactly in between our places of residence, it was close enough.

This, I answered, was a great idea. As these things usually are, the reunion was in August – perfect for me. Summer school was over and the fall term hadn't begun. So I had no classes to teach. Of course, I would have to tell everybody my whereabouts for a couple of days and that I hadn't been kidnapped by aliens, but that was my only obligation. We agreed we'd meet at the hotel bar once we got settled.

Bill gave me the website for the reunion – it couldn't be anything as outdated as a mailing address or a phone number. But in no time, I had made the reservations. It was easy as pie, although I still was not comfortable sending my credit card number off into cyberspace. Call me paranoid, but I briefly wondered if the whole thing might be a scam – not really worth the effort for my money, but multiply that by the number of '61 graduates... Naw. From our correspondence,

Bill had known too much about me. But what if Bill was the scam-master?

"Oh, quit," I told myself out loud.

Imagine my surprise when the airport cab pulled up at the hotel. It was very nice in a modern high-rise sort of way, but the location bothered me. It was right where good old Woodrow Wilson had been. Somebody had torn down that three-story red-brick Georgian structure and replaced it with this steel-and-glass edifice. Where the white stone lettering proudly proclaiming *Woodrow Wilson High School, built 1945* had dominated the entryway, there was a big ugly neon sign with the name of the hotel on it.

"Go Bearcats," I mumbled, walking into the lobby.

As I checked in with the friendly desk clerk, my mind wandered. Almost in this very spot – which used to be the boys restroom – Bill and I had pantsed Benny the Nerd. But my room turned out to be nice so, being early, I took a nap. I'd probably need all my strength for that partying bunch of '61s.

Waking a couple of hours before the big gathering was scheduled, I showered, dressed, slipped on a sport coat, and headed out to find Bill.

Back in the spacious lobby, I noted that to the left was the conference/banquet room where I figured the gathering would take place. On the right, just past the entrance, was the "Bar & Grill." I wondered if that was a nod to temperance.

On the interior, the Bar & Grill was clearly fashioned after an Irish pub — a dark Irish pub. I stood waiting for my eyes to adjust. After a few moments, I could see that a woman already sitting at the bar and I were the only customers. So much for those wild Bearcat party warriors. Not wanting to seem untoward or unfriendly, I took a stool two removed from the woman and ordered a beer to wait for Bill.

Two carefully nursed beers later, still no Bill. I wondered if he'd missed his flight, or maybe just changed his mind.

"Here for the reunion?" I addressed the woman.

She turned and studied me. "Actually, yes. You?"

"You bet. Class of '61. Errrah!" I gave the Bearcat growl.

She smiled. "My name's Lolita Lock, but that's not what they called me in high school."

Moving beside her, I introduced myself and we shook hands. This woman did not even look vaguely familiar. Tall, pleasant figure, beautiful raven hair, handsome face – surely I should have remembered her. On the other hand, it had been fifty years. No telling what a person might have looked like so long ago. I was pretty certain I didn't resemble the scrawny teenager I was in high school.

I wanted to ask her what she was called back then, but since she hadn't volunteered the name, maybe it was something she had spent years trying to shake. In fact, knowing she had to be sixty-something, it was pretty clear that she had invested heavily in maintaining her youth. Dyed hair, probably a face-lift, no telling what else. Whatever. She looked good for her age. I almost forgot about Bill. So we prattled comfortably, as people do who have nothing to prove and something to share.

We spoke of many things we had experienced together long ago. All things considered, I couldn't imagine why I didn't recognize her. Time flew and I became aware that the appointed hour for the gathering was upon us. Still no Bill.

"I guess we ought to go in. I was supposed to meet someone here, but…"

"You did meet someone here." She smiled.

"Yeah. And it was a real pleasure, but I was supposed to meet an old friend. I guess something happened to him," I said.

"You did meet your old friend here." She stared into my eyes.

"No. I mean..." I paused.

"I know what you mean. Do you know what I mean?" Her eyes seemed to sparkle as a tight smile materialized on her lips. Not Mona Lisa quality, but interesting just the same.

Grappling to understand, explanations rattled through my head like the tumblers in a sophisticated lock. Finally they fell into place. I opened my mouth. Nothing came out. I shut it again like the dog on the old Nestle's commercial.

"Yeah, buddy. It's me. Your ol' pal Bill."

Well, just what does a person say to that? There were definitely some mixed feelings, like when you see the human face melt off the monster in the horror movies. I mean, just a few minutes ago, somewhere in the back of my mind were thoughts of maybe trying to maneuver this woman into the sack. I guess it's good that he/she came clean early, otherwise

I'd have been in for a *real* shock. This feeling was more of a numbness – as if I woke up in the wrong dimension where up was down and down was up. I couldn't think of anything to say. The words to *Lola* ran through my mind: "Lo, Lo, Lo-la, Lola." *Oh my God*, I thought.

"Are you pissed off?" Bill/Lolita asked. She/he seemed to be genuinely concerned.

"No… I don't think so. But what do I call you? Are you a he or a she?" It was all I could think of to say.

"I'm a real live she, and you can call me Lo," she said, and then began to laugh. "That's all you want to know?"

"Why?" I asked the question like *Am I asking the right question?* But as soon as I asked, I knew I shouldn't have because I knew what she was going to say. The usual about being a woman trapped in a man's body, yada, yada, yada.

"Is that why your wife left?" I asked, when she finished her explanation.

"Yeah. Peg is a good woman, but really. Nobody vows to love, honor, and obey if your husband turns into a woman. The kids aren't crazy about it, either. At least I didn't run off and make the change while the kids were growing up. They were all married with kids. And actually, Peg and I hadn't gotten along for a long time. So if I was ever gonna do it, it was time."

"So," I said.

"So," she said, and paused. "Wanna take me to the dance?"

Fifty years ago, I would have run, not walked, out of this situation. I might have even felt challenged by my old friend's existence. Things were different now. Our whole society was more tolerant. Besides that, I lived a thousand miles away and didn't know anybody who lived in this town anymore. And at sixty-eight-years-old, I guess I could go to a high school reunion with my best boyhood friend – even if he had changed sexes.

"Why the hell not?" I smiled, meaning it.

Walking out, *not* arm in arm, I stopped and looked at her.

"One thing, Lo," I said, reversing my normal approach. "When this is over, you go to your own room."

She chuckled – a little too deeply.

SOME THINGS NEVER CHANGE

Samford Highman retired to Pensacola Beach, Florida, when he left the Great South Dakota Security Company after forty years in their accounting department. He only knew he did not want any more cold.

Sam had originally considered retiring to one of the western states, notably Colorado. But he found the age mix not to his liking at all. The whole state seemed to be populated with people who regarded senior citizens as extraneous to the real world, people who grew impatient with seniors when they took time to order food, consider options, or just drive their cars. "Do it fast" seemed to be the watch phrase. Older people just got in the way. Sam wondered if they had parents. He hoped they'd remember their intolerance when they got older, but they probably wouldn't. Besides, it was cold.

South Florida stayed too hot. South Texas was almost as hot and had too many Mexicans. It wasn't that Sam didn't like Mexicans; he just didn't want to be in the minority. But Pensacola seemed just right – not too hot, except maybe in August; not too cold, except maybe in January; and a real American cultural melting pot. Pensacola had a nice blend of whites and blacks, military and rednecks, affluent and not so affluent, but most importantly old and young.

In Pensacola, there were lots of "cotton heads," as he liked to call seniors for obvious reasons. In fact, the old seemed to outnumber the young by a good margin. But the young had a healthy respect for their elders. And everybody was friendly. That was important, too. Sam was lonely. His wife of thirty years had just waltzed out the door one day. Said she didn't want to waste the rest of her life on Sam. And that was that. Sam was glad he never had any children with her, but a good daughter would be nice now to take care of him in his old age.

But no matter; he wasn't exactly decrepit. *Hell, I'm almost as good as I ever was*, he often thought. He might not have a wife or a daughter, but there were lots of widows – especially younger widows – who'd be happy to take care of Sam. He had his retirement money, a nice Mustang convertible, and even a neat little bachelor pad overlooking the sugar-white sand and the emerald-green water of the Gulf of Mexico. Sam was a catch. At least, that's the way Sam looked at it.

This day, Sam was engaged in one of his favorite things to do. He liked to bar hop on the beach. It wasn't just the cold beer, although that was nice too. It was the camaraderie of sitting around some little bar with locals and tourists, especially the women. Today, Sam had picked the Sand Bar as a first stop.

Sean Terry was Pensacola-local to the core. Twenty-one, Sean had graduated from Pensacola High School and managed to spend three years en route to an associates degree at Pensacola State College. One of these days, he supposed he would get that bachelors degree in something.

Clearly Sean wasn't anxious to go anywhere, but if you asked him, he could go on for an hour or so about how there were no opportunities for young people in Pensacola and how he couldn't wait to take his shot somewhere like Atlanta or Dallas or maybe even Denver. Although he was probably correct in his estimate of opportunity in Pensacola, he was really quite happy to be right where he was. But it was hard to score with some tourist chick if he admitted his ambition in life was to make enough money to fish and carouse when he wasn't taking – or cutting – some class at the college.

His parents had a garage apartment and they had agreed to pay his tuition and let him live there as long as he gave the appearance of trying to get a degree. His salary as a part-time bartender in town paid enough for the rest. For transportation, he still drove the classic Cadillac convertible he'd begged for and gotten as a present for high school graduation.

Sean also liked to surf in the usually placid waters of the gulf. And he looked the part with his blond hair, lean muscular body, and dark tan. In fact, that's exactly what he had done this morning instead of making an English literature class. Now he was heading to an island bar for a cold beer and to see who he could find to occupy the rest of his day. Normally his bar *du jour* would be Hooters or Bamboo Willie's with the younger set, but this a Wednesday and things wouldn't get rockin' until much later. For this afternoon, the Sand Bar seemed right.

Coming into the Sand Bar from the heat and the dazzling glare of the beach world, it took a bit for Sam's eyes to adjust to the relative dark of the bar.

This was not the conveniently dark rendezvous where couples with the wrong partner met for an afternoon. In fact, it wasn't that dark. It was just the relative difference that caused Sam to squint. In no time, he could make out the worn horseshoe-shaped wooden bar flanked with stools upholstered in aging red plastic. Other than a few non-shaded windows, light was provided by a variety of neon beer advertisements. If a person really focused on his surroundings, which sometimes happened in awkward moments, the random designs of water spots would materialize on the ceiling. There was a jukebox, but the music was set on low. This was a bar for drinking and talking, not dancing and being seen. Under its prior owner, the Sand Bar had styled itself as "an adult daycare center."

Even at this hour, there were several of the regular customers sitting near the door engaged in their drink of choice and light conversation. It was a little early for heavy philosophy or heated political debate. Sam nodded at every-one. They all knew each others' first names.

But what caught Sam's attention was the lone woman on the far side of the bar, politely separated from the regulars. Sam guessed somewhere between forty and fifty years of age, she had long black hair and, from what Sam could see, a pleasing figure. Sam figured she was a tourist since he hadn't seen her around before.

"Miller Lite," said Sam to the bartender as he made his way over toward the new woman.

Sam would let fate determine how close he would get to the woman by the barman's placement of the beer. If he was lucky, a couple of seats down would be best – not too close, but not so far away that conversation would be diffi-cult. He was lucky.

After satisfying himself that the beer at the Sand Bar was still the coldest on the island, Sam half turned and said, "New to the beach?"

"Does it show?" The woman gave a slight smile.

"Naw. Just hadn't seen you around and it beats 'Hi, what's your sign?'" Sam took a chance. The lady either want-ed to play or not, and she'd let him know right away.

Her smile hinted at intrigue. Sam moved over one seat closer.

It was just about this time when Sean Terry showed up at the Sand Bar. Sean was not the sort of person who sought to be innocuous. He was not a person in the crowd you gradually became aware of. When Sean entered a room, everybody knew it.

"Howdy, folks. Sean's the name, cold beer's the game." He gave his best "I'm just here to have fun; no harm meant" smile. Then to the barman, "Give the new guy a Bud." Downing it quickly with a flourish, he exclaimed, "That tasted just like another one. How 'bout it, barkeep?"

The group at the door closed ranks and went back to their conversation – probably about fishing. Sam was attempting to do the same, *sans* fishing, when he felt the presence of the new arrival at his elbow.

"Hey, dude," Sean said, directing his attention to Sam. "Nice to see a man bonding with his daughter." Again the smile.

"Look, buddy, we're just tryin' to have a quiet conversation here. Why don't you go hang ten or something?" Sam was neither enchanted nor amused by Sean's smile and wit.

"Well, fuck you if you can't take a joke." Sean's winning smile turned into a sneer.

Sam had had just enough beer to feel a lot more powerful than he really was. He dismounted the barstool.

The strange woman had seen this drill before and wanted no part of it. One guy was too old. One guy was too young. Neither held promise for her. "Boys, boys," she barked, moving between the would-be combatants. "Try to behave like gentlemen." It wasn't that she intended to break up a fight. The problem was that Sam and Sean were blocking her path. Making room between them, she walked out the door.

Both men watched agape.

"Nice going, Pop." It was Sean who first recovered.

"'Nice going,' my ass. You're the one who cut in, prick." Sam's anger headed north again.

This exchange was followed by something resembling a weird dance as both men glared and stuck out their chests, swaying in each other's direction. Maybe this was bluff or maybe it presaged a genuine fistfight; that would remain unknown.

"KABLAM!" The noise resonated in the small bar, stopping both men in mid-pose. The bartender had slammed down a cudgel, kept under the bar for just such purposes, with enough force that the group near the front could feel the vibration on the bar rail.

"You assholes just ran off a payin' customer. I don't give a damn what you do to each other, but you take it out of here right now." He punctuated his order with a wave of the club.

"But…" Sam started.

"I don't want to hear it. Out. Now. Both of you."

Both men turned and stalked toward the door. Sam, noting Sean's youth and brawn, ducked into the bathroom instead. He hoped that Sean was not intent on continuing their encounter and took his time. If Sean was in the parking lot, this could be bad. Sam considered going back into the bar, but then he remembered the woman was gone. The angry bartender with a club gave him pause as well. So out he crept into the blazing sunshine, wondering if he could find anything to use to even up the odds in case Sean was waiting.

However, Sean really wasn't a fighter. When the old

man didn't immediately follow him out of the bar, he hopped in the Cadillac, next to his surfboard, and drove off in the direction of town. Maybe he'd get something to eat, clean up, and try his luck later. *What a jerk*, he thought, as he flashed a smile at two bikini-clad beach strollers.

Now rolling toward town, Sean, wind blowing through his hair, was at one with his world. He had already mentally moved on from the incident in the bar.

But Sam had not forgotten the little dust-up. Sam was busy ruminating about and replaying the confrontation and what led up to it.

Man, that woman was warming up to me. Maybe a few more beers, perhaps a late lunch, then, with a little luck, back to show her my place. If it hadn't been for that goddam surfer-boy, I had it made. Sam knew that realistically, he wouldn't have been able to prevail in a one-on-one with Blondie. He knew Florida had a concealed weapon law and wondered if he could get a permit. If he'd had a gun today, it would have been real different. He could see it in his head.

Blondie walks in and makes a crack about Sam being with his daughter. But instead of coming back all pissed off, he'd turn toward the surfer, smile and let his jacket open just enough to display his .357 mag-

num. "*Son,*" *he'd say, real cool.* "*I think you're disturbing the lady. You need to move on.*" *Then, just in case the surfer hadn't seen the big gun, Sam would look down at it and say* "*Doncha think?*"

Sam could see the look on the boy's face as the boy backed out making that palms-out gesture meaning "*Be cool*" *and saying* "*Sorry, sir. My mistake.*"

Sam smiled at that thought – unaware that, being lost in fantasy, he was tailgating the car in front of him.

Sean, although being at one with his world, noticed that someone in a Mustang convertible was dangerously close to his rear bumper. Peering into his rearview mirror, he recognized the Mustang's driver. "It's that goddam ol' man. Fuck!"

His first inclination was to hit his brakes. *That'd fix the old fart,* he thought. *If you rear-end somebody, it's always your fault.* At least, that's what he'd heard, but he couldn't remember where. *Maybe that's not right. Maybe that was just one of the other surfers talking.* He didn't want his classic car damaged by some cheap Ford, especially if he might have to pay for it. He moved to the right lane.

Sam, who hadn't been paying any attention, passed Sean without a thought, not even looking in his direction as he went by.

The deal at the bar hadn't meant much to Sean, but then the tailgating, and now blowing past like Sean was some peon. That was too much. Sean moved to the left lane and hit the gas.

One thing about the old eight-cylinders, when you put the pedal down, the car moved. Now it was Sean who was riding Sam's tail. Unfortunately for Sean, Sam paid him no mind. He was still lost in thought. Getting no satisfaction, after a while Sean honked – loud and long.

That got Sam's attention. But of course he didn't know it was his former adversary. He just realized he'd been daydreaming and probably blocking traffic. Even though the long blast on the horn behind him was irritating, Sam, recognizing he was probably at fault, moved to the right.

Sean hit the gas again. Now they were running side-by-side. Sean glowered at Sam. Sam, back in his inner world, paid no attention. That made Sean even madder. Again he hit the horn long and loud.

Now what? Sam thought as his anger flashed and he looked toward the source of the annoyance. It was that damn kid... and he was giving Sam the finger and mouthing the words "fuck you." Before he had time to worry, Sam returned the favor.

It was about this time that both cars were stopped by the first red light coming into the city. There they sat, side by side, glaring. When the light turned green, both drivers hit the gas, both thinking *By God, we'll see who's the best man.*

The Mustang, new and fast, squealed out like a bullet. The old Cadillac hiccupped and died. Even though Sam didn't realize there was no contest, as the Mustang's speedometer hit sixty, Sam looked in his rearview mirror hoping for the worst. And that's what he saw. Not Sean, but one of Pensacola's finest, takedown lights blazing and siren blaring. Sam pulled to the curb and banged his head on the steering wheel in frustration.

Recovering his composure, Sam looked to his left just in time to see a wildly laughing Sean ride by bobbing in the seat and again giving him the finger. It was just after that that Sean, mocking Sam instead of looking at the road, hit the light pole.

BEARS REPEATING

In the United States, there are many breathtakingly beautiful natural phenomena to be witnessed. Most Americans, unless they are terminally afflicted by the steel-and-glass megalopolis myopia prevalent on the east and west coasts, could probably name a dozen such places right off hand.

On anyone's list, though, should be the Colorado Rocky Mountains in summer – the raw and jagged peaks descending to the emerald velvet of the pines and aspen enclosed under the endless depth of incomparable blue sky crowned with the single dazzling jewel of sunlight. The air is warm unless the observer chances to linger in the lee of some jutting edifice where the chill of winter seems to hold perpetual domain.

I didn't put it exactly that way to Jimmy. What I said was "Neat place, huh?"

Jimmy is my ten-year-old grandson. To carry on any kind of conversation with Jimmy, it is necessary to translate thoughts into the jargon of the pre-teen, which can be frighteningly close to the incomprehensible argot of the full-blown teenager.

"You mean badass?" he replied and smiled, watching closely for my reaction.

Of course, my first impulse was to slip into parental mode and explain that "ass" was not a word that he should be using. Besides that, "badass" – if it's a recognized word at all – in my world is a noun or an adjective used to describe a violent and dangerous person. However, Jimmy's father was my child; not Jimmy. So as far as I was concerned, my job was to be a role model, as opposed to a teacher and disciplinarian.

"I guess you could put it that way," I said without adding "if you want to be judged as foul-mouthed and inarticulate, unable to conform the English language to meet your needs."

We continued to walk the trail of gently scented pine

needles, with me pointing out things of interest and beauty. Jimmy seemed to be paying attention... marginally. I wondered how a person, even a beginning person, could be exposed to nature in her glory and somehow be bored. Perhaps nature appreciation was an acquired taste. Perhaps in a world of computer graphics unfolding in nanoseconds, the earth appeared slow and dowdy by comparison. Perhaps that's why Jimmy's parents had decided Jimmy needed to "bond" with Grampa in Colorado.

"Are there really bears up here?" Jimmy asked, apparently tired of plants and peaks.

"You bet," I said.

"Will they eat you?"

I thought about that. "Not usually."

"That means sometimes they will, right?"

"Yeah, but our bears eat mostly berries and bugs and an occasional small animal. Humans aren't really something they're much interested in eating. Humans usually get hurt by bears when they surprise them or get between a mother bear and her cubs." I didn't mention that a bear will eat just about anything, and he might eat a human who had attacked him for some reason.

"What would you do if you saw a bear? I'd run or climb a tree."

"You know, that *sounds* like a good thing to do," I started, not wanting to say that those two methods of evading bears would pretty much get you killed. "But bears are real good climbers and they're much faster runners than humans."

Jimmy thought about that for a while. "So what do you do if you see a bear? Are you packin' heat?"

"No." I stifled a laugh. *Too many gangster movies*, I guessed. "I'm not packin' heat. What you do out here hiking is try to make noise – like we're talking. That way the bear can hear you before you come up on him. Bears will run away from humans if they have a chance."

"But what if they don't hear you?"

"Well, then you slowly back away until you get out of the bear's sight. Odds are, once he can't see you anymore, he'll go on about his business."

"Oh." Jimmy furrowed his brow, likely imagining an encounter with a bear.

"Hey, look at that," I said, pointing to a brown glob mixed with berries on the trail in front of us. "Do you know what that is?"

Jimmy looked closely for a moment. Then he canted his eyes in my direction and said with a satisfied smile, "Shit."

Surely my son and his wife did not countenance such language. Jimmy must be testing limits with me, and he had just found one. "Nice people, like you and me, don't use that sort of language. It's called 'scat.' Do you know what kind of sh… scat it is?"

Jimmy's look was confused. *Why would anyone care?* he must have thought.

I preempted whatever he was about to say. "You were asking about bears. That's one of the ways we know if there are bears around. You can tell it's a bear by the little berries in it because that's what bears eat."

"Oh." He blinked and looked closely again. "Wow." Apparently bear scat was something of serious interest to a ten-year-old.

"Can you tell how close the bear is?"

"Well…" I weighed the pros and cons of this discussion. "You can get an idea by how much it's dried or how warm it is." I hoped Jimmy did not want me to stick my finger in it.

"Neat. So how close is he?"

"Well, I can't say exactly." I was not going to stick my finger in it even if it meant losing face. "But it looks fresh, so he's around here somewhere. He's probably already heard us and gone back to wherever he lives." *No point in scaring the boy,* I thought. Then I added, "It's gettin' kinda late, but there's a neat waterfall just around the bend up here. After we take a look at it, we'll head back."

After a few steps, Jimmy stopped dead. "What was that?"

I hadn't heard anything. "Probably a bird in the underbrush. Don't worry." Just in case, though, I increased my volume.

Jimmy looked at me suspiciously.

As we rounded the corner to view the waterfall, it was me who stopped dead. Not twenty yards in front of us was a large bear and one cub. Maybe that was good. Maybe not. Maybe there was another cub somewhere. My heart raced as cold fear coursed through my brain. If animals can really smell fear, that ol' bear surely had a lock on me.

"Jimmy," I said, trying for vocal control. "Give me your hand slowly and don't run."

The bear regarded us in a way that could have been

either boredom or her I'm-about-to-eat-you look. I stood as tall as I could and began backing away in slow motion, trying to keep myself between Jimmy and the bear's line of sight without tripping over him.

I thought things were going well when the cub apparently noticed us and decided to investigate. This was not good at all. If I shouted at the cub, mom might take that as a threat. If I did nothing, the cub would be sniffing our pants-legs in no time at all. I slowed my pace of retreat. Now mom began to follow her cub.

Suddenly from somewhere beyond the mother came the cry of what could only be a mountain lion. The bear wheeled and rose to her full height. The cub continued un-perturbed toward us.

Maybe the park ranger would have had a better sug-gestion, but he wasn't there. I threw my walking stick at the cub, pulled Jimmy to me, and urgently whispered "Run." The mother bear seemed to be otherwise occupied and I didn't give a damn what the cub might do. We ran as fast as an old guy and a ten-year-old could run down a mountain.

We skipped the scenic route and in no time we were in my front yard, panting and still looking over our shoulders.

As near as I could tell, neither ever gave chase. My guess is there was a second cub that was being menaced by the mountain lion. That was a bigger threat than a man and a boy who were backing away.

Sweating as we entered the house, Jimmy, wide-eyed, exclaimed, "Gramma, we were chased by a giant bear. We had to run like crazy or she'd have eaten us."

"Oh, Jimmy. You're spoofin' me," countered my wife, watching me.

"Nope. That bear was badass," I responded.

My wife's jaw dropped.

Jimmy smiled.

DEAL OF A LIFETIME

If nothing else, Noah Rich had been lucky in life – at least, pretty lucky.

On the one hand, his existence had not been marred by major tragedy. On the other, his course had not led even close to vast wealth and celebrity.

He had married after college and produced two healthy kids. With just better than mediocre college grades, Noah had stumbled into a reasonably interesting job with a major corporation back in the day when a person could spend his entire working life with the same employer and move comfortably up the company ladder to a nice retirement.

Noah had done just that and now lived in Florida with his wife. He occupied his time with golf and volunteer work, as did his wife. Occasionally his children, also relatively lucky in life, would come to visit. By most standards, Noah should have been content to fade off into the sunset, completing the cycle of his slice of Americana.

However, Noah did not necessarily agree with the popular view of the life and times of Noah Rich. He did not consider his state of being as the perfect end to a perfect life, and this dissonance had begun even before he had retired.

When he passed age forty, Noah became vaguely aware that it was unlikely he would ever be the President of the United States, throw a touchdown pass in the Super Bowl, or spend time on his yacht in the Caribbean with some movie starlet. It dawned on him that his vision was fading and his hairline receding. But what could he do? He bought reading glasses and some new miracle hair-restorer that didn't work and went on about the business of the American dream.

From fifty to sixty-five, he ignored the whole aging thing mostly because physically and mentally he didn't seem to be losing anything – except hair, which he could style in a comb-over.

His real dissatisfaction came with retirement and the move to Florida. Why he had ever quit work and moved to

Florida, he didn't know. Actually, he knew why he quit work. He hit the mandatory retirement age for his company. But why Florida? He decided he had been unduly influenced by his wife and friends. It had been presented as "the sunshine state," the land of the legendary Fountain of Youth, the state of the golden agers. Now his thought was *Phooey. More like the heat and rain state populated by old people. Home of the "senior discount." Clearly, if there's a youth fountain, nobody in Florida has found it.*

However, being surrounded by old people wasn't *per se* the worst part. Apparently it was contagious. He was aging, too, like the remnants of sand running through an hourglass.

First, it was his back. Then his knees, his neck, and his feet. His curly blond hair was a thing of the past. Only gray clumps on the sides and back remained. And bifocals, for God's sake – could trifocals be far away? Not to mention the wrinkles. Once he caught a glimpse of himself in a mirror and, to his horror, he momentarily found himself wondering *Who is that old man?* He almost shuffled when he walked – his former military posture now bowed. His first thought in the morning stillness when he opened his eyes was *What part of me is gonna go out today?* All his new friends had "M.D." after their last name.

All those things were bad enough, but worse was that they led to an unavoidable conclusion: *I am truly getting old.*

At forty and fifty, even sixty-five, it was easy to somehow disregard the fact of mortality. Why that was, he didn't know. Everybody past the age of reason knows that no one comes out of life alive. Maybe it was that at younger ages the very act of fully experiencing life leads to a self-delusion that life will go on forever.

But toward the end, the evidence begins to relentlessly build that the end is coming up pretty quick and there's nothing you can do to stop it. Almost daily, it seemed, he could look back and recall what was no longer physically possible – running, walking fast, mounting the stairs two at a time. He didn't even want to think about sex. How many trips to the closet, only to discover you've forgotten why you're there, did it take to establish that the ability to focus was fading? Everything winding down to… what?

The ultimate for Noah was thinking about a world in existence without the great and wonderful "I" in its center to experience it. *What of world events, of people I've watched begin and develop? How can I not be there to see closure? The advent of miracles*

I've never even dreamed of?

These were the thoughts that dampened his spirits and preoccupied his waking hours to the point of despair. It seemed so critically unfair. Sure other people died. But that was them, not the "I." Noah actually wept as he stood on his balcony overlooking the Gulf of Mexico. *I would give anything to be young again* – his mental plea so intense, he startled himself.

It also startled his wife Margie, who'd been observing Noah on the balcony and noticed the look on his face – as if he'd just taken a big bite of a raw onion. Of late, Margie had decided that Noah really did need watching. He had become an absolute wet blanket. He wasn't even fun to watch TV with – much less play golf. And he never wanted to get together with friends. It was Margie's analysis that Noah was probably getting Alzheimer's. And this conclusion did not so much cause Margie grief as it pissed her off. She did not want to be stuck by herself caring for a vegetable. Two kids had been enough. She didn't bargain for a third, not at this age anyway.

The glorious sunset was fading, turning the sky from brilliant red to dark purple, when Margie decided that she would mix her own cocktail. Noah could just stand out there in the dark, if that's what he wanted to do.

Noah was quite happy with the dark. It suited his mood. As the turtle-friendly lights of the condominium blinked on, he noticed a man standing on the adjacent balcony. Noah wondered if the man had seen him crying and made ready to make a hasty retreat inside.

"Hi, Noah," said the man. "Why so down?" The man's voice was oddly comforting.

For some time now, Noah had not felt very social, and speaking to an unannounced stranger was not usually to his liking. But Noah felt he needed to talk to someone. He'd avoided his friends – and that included Margie, who teased him unmercifully when he complained of aging. Perhaps this person was a kindred spirit.

"Life," said Noah flatly.

To Noah's surprise, the man agreed – even seemed sympathetic. "Yes, I know. It seems so unfair. Just when a man could really appreciate life, it's time to say goodbye."

It felt good to hear someone say what he'd been thinking. A world-weary expression spread across Noah's face as he replied, "But I guess there's nothing you can do about it." His shoulders sagged.

That was when the man smiled – rather brightly for the occasion, Noah thought. "Maybe. Maybe not." The man's smile was now accompanied by a knowing look.

Wonderful. Just wonderful. Noah almost threw up his hands in frustration. *Here I am in a terrible depression and a cryogenics salesman comes to comfort me.*

"I'm not selling anything, Noah," the man said.

That stopped Noah in his tracks. *How does he know what I'm thinking? And how does he know my name is Noah?*

"Think about it, Noah. What was your last thought before I... appeared?"

After discarding thoughts he'd had about the sunset, his wife, and his expandable pants being too tight, it came to him. "That I would give," he hesitated, "anything to be young again." Somehow that one word – "anything" – took on an odd significance.

"That's the one, Noah." The man pointed his index finger like a gun as he gave Noah a probing stare. "Would you really?"

Noah glanced over his shoulder wondering, *Where the hell is Margie when I actually need her to interrupt a conversation?* "I...

I don't know, really," he stammered. He tried to clear his head with a mental shake. "But then, it really doesn't matter, now does it?"

"Actually, Noah, it does." The man paused poignantly. "You think about it. I'll be around."

Noah turned his head to break the uncomfortable eye-lock they had maintained. When he again looked for the man, he was gone. Despite the Florida heat, Noah felt a chill as he hurried inside.

For the remainder of the evening, Noah suppressed all thought of the strange man and what he could have meant. That included not mentioning the odd occurrence to Margie, who had been studying him peculiarly for a while now. Telling her about a guy appearing on the balcony babbling nonsense was all she would need to conclude that it was time for Noah to visit the doctor. But later that night, Noah lay awake in bed pondering the meaning of the man's appearance.

Clearly the guy had something in mind about regaining youth. Noah was not unread. He knew about people who had allegedly traded their soul for youth. But that was just fiction. And that was with the devil. This guy didn't look like the devil – at least not any devil Noah had ever seen. But then, all the devils Noah had ever seen were in paintings or movies. As far as Noah knew, there weren't any snapshots or documentaries on the devil. Well, maybe the Bible said something about the devil. Noah wasn't sure how a work like the Bible was classified, though.

But what if that guy was the devil? Maybe the devil dressed and looked pretty much like everyone else. Showing up in a red cape and pointy horns probably wouldn't go over very well in modern America. So, just for argument's sake, let's say the guy was someone who had the power to give back youth. Say he was the devil. What would he want? Noah instantly asked himself, *What would I be willing to give?* Then he smiled to himself. *What wouldn't I be willing to give to be twenty-five years old again?*

Noah tried to weigh all the pros and cons, but he couldn't come up with any cons – and the pros were dazzling. It was with that thought that he was overtaken by sleep.

The dawning of a new day caught Noah puzzling over the occurrence of the prior night. *Who was that guy?* Then an uncomfortable thought struck like a thump on the forehead. *What if there wasn't any guy? What if it was some kind of hallucination brought on by a desperate need to avoid the grim reaper – like when people dying of thirst see – even feel – cool ponds of water?* Then a more distressing idea formed. *Is this just another part of old age?* Noah pulled the cover over his head and morphed into the fetal position, trying very hard to blot out all thought.

"Noah," came the voice of Margie. "It's wakie wakie time."

My God, my God, what have I done to deserve this? he inwardly moaned, but said, "Yes, dear. Coming."

Dragging himself to the brightly lit breakfast nook, Noah winced. "Can't we shut the blinds, Margie?"

"No, we can't shut the blinds." Margie dropped a plate of scrambled eggs from about two inches above the tabletop, which startled Noah to attention. "We spent a bunch of money to have a bright little breakfast nook, and I'm not shuttin' the blinds." She paused, then continued on a different line of irritation. "How long has it been since you shaved? You look like an old goat."

A scene from an old James Cagney movie flashed through his mind – the one where Cagney shoved a grapefruit-half in Mae Clarke's face at the breakfast table. But Noah didn't have a grapefruit-half, and if he threw the plate of eggs, he'd probably just have to clean it up. The whole spat scene was just too much trouble. Instead he pushed his chair away from the table. "I'm not very hungry, Margie. I think I'll go" *slit my throat*, he thought, but said, "shave."

As long as he was shaving, he decided he might as well shower. Moving at the speed of flowing ketchup, the whole process took about an hour. Toweling himself dry, he heard Margie's melodious voice.

"Are you ever coming out of there?"

Noah thought the question over. *It might be nice to stay in the bathroom forever.*

But before he could answer, Margie continued. "Well, I'm going shopping. Do you need anything?"

"No, dear," he said, and stood naked waiting for the sound that would signal a measure of tranquility. The door slammed. Noah sighed, opted against going back to bed, and began the rigorous process of dressing himself.

Thirty minutes or so later, Noah clip-clopped into the living area of the condominium. Lace-up shoes had presented too much of a hassle, so he was wearing his house shoes that made a soft clopping noise as he walked. Ruling out TV as too insipid, reading as too challenging, standing in the middle of the room staring at nothing as just too weird, he made his way to the balcony. This wasn't a particularly good idea. The Gulf of Mexico was beautiful, but if he looked straight down, five stories below he could see people having a good time, *young people* having a good time, *young people* having a good time without Noah. As Noah's face sunk like heated wax, he heard a familiar voice.

"Life got you down, again? Too much marital bliss?" came the voice from what he assumed was the next condo over.

It was then that Noah realized that there wasn't "a next condo over." As well as the breakfast nook, they had paid additional money for a corner unit, and to his left was nothing but air. Noah's head jerked in the direction of the voice. There, not five feet away, was the man Noah had met the night before, but this time, instead of leaning over the railing, the man was just sitting… on nothing.

"OK to come aboard?" The man canted his head to match his query.

Noah couldn't say anything, just nodded his head vigorously. He hoped the people frolicking on the beach weren't looking up. *Nothing starts a good rumor better than being seen talking to a man floating on air.*

"Give our little conversation any thought?" the man said.

"Eh, yes. Eh, how'd you do that? What's your name?" Noah stammered.

"Oh, I don't think names are all that important, and I think you know who I am, don't you, Noah?"

"Well, yes. I guess I do. You're... eh." Noah didn't want to make the devil mad. Who knew what a mad devil might do? "What do you like to be called?"

"Well, I was always partial to the name God, but that name seems to be taken. All the other names you've heard – Beelzebub, Lucifer, Satan, Old Scratch, yada, yada, yada – have a certain negative connotation. So why don't you call me Jake. I've liked the name ever since my... shall we say 'my friend' Steve McQueen used the name in a movie."

Noah didn't use the name. "Jake" didn't sound right for the devil. In fact, Noah didn't know what to say. So he didn't say anything.

But Jake did. "So I guess the question is: What's it gonna be, Noah? Life forever at your chosen age?" Jake looked over the railing at the frolickers. "Or more 'golden years' followed by who knows what?" Jake kind of flicked his eyebrows up and smiled tightly.

After a brief silence, Noah said, "What's the catch?" Of course, he knew what the catch was, but he wanted to make sure. *Who knows? Things may have changed.*

Jake grinned broadly. "Oh, I'm sure you know what the *quid pro quo* is. Just like it's always been. You get eternal youth; I get your soul when you decide to give it up."

Noah mulled that over a bit. *If a person had eternal youth, why would he ever give it up to go burn in hell?* But then he had a second thought and asked, "What if a bus runs over me to-morrow? You know – an accident?"

"Welll…" Jake stretched the word. "Stuff happens. But it's still a chance thing. If I were to interfere in the way of things, the deal would be null and void."

Noah looked smug. He wasn't so easily fooled.

"Consider this, though," Jake posited. "You've lived seventy-something years so far and haven't been run over by a bus yet. The odds are still the same. It's the same principle as flipping a coin. And… I know something that you don't. Maybe today's your last day anyway. Maybe you're gonna be my guest one way or the other." Jake let that sink in. "Plus, hell's not what you've heard. No torture. No fire and brimstone. That's just propaganda from the other side. And doin' it this way is kinda like early admission to college. Sign up now and you can be on my team when you get there."

Noah was puzzled and looked it.

"Look. Hell's not that bad even if you're drafted. But if you enlist, then it's really pretty good. You help me out – say on something like this – and you get whatever you want in hell."

"If what you say is true, why does everybody sweat going to… well, you know."

"Yeah, I know. There is one thing."

"Aha. What's that?" Again Noah looked smug.

"Well…" Jake's expression was bored. "You don't get to see… you know, Him." His expression brightened. "But that's not so bad. I haven't seen Him in centuries and it doesn't bother me a bit. What's the big deal? Has it bothered you in seventy-odd years?"

Noah considered, then said, "So the deal is I get eternal youth unless I die accidentally or something like that. If I do die, or just get tired of being eternally youthful and give it up, I go to work for you. That's the whole thing? No tricks?"

"That's it. No tricks. No hidden clauses. Straight up."

Jake looked earnest – or at least as earnest as the devil can look. "In fact, here you go." Jake produced a document that looked official but was singed around the edges. "A contract in writing."

Noah took the piece of paper, which felt slightly warm even in the Florida heat. "When do I have to decide?"

Jake looked offended, as if he were thinking *You need time to consider such a super deal?* "I can give you a day. But that's it. Same time, same place tomorrow. No decision, no deal. Then it's whatever you've got left and wherever you're supposed to go after."

Noah nodded solemnly and, turning to go inside, muttered, "OK. See you then… Jake."

Once sitting inside the air-conditioned comfort of his condo with a nice cup of tea, Noah realized he didn't really have much to consider. There was nothing in his life that he more than faintly cared about. Sure, he loved Margie and the kids – kinda. He knew, though, that it wouldn't be six months after he was gone before he was mostly forgotten. Margie would inherit enough to keep her in the style to which she was accustomed. She would fall easily into the rhythm of the other widow ladies – and there were a ton of them around –

playing cards, shopping, chasing what few old guys were left. Basically she would be much happier without him. And the kids, they'd get a nice bump in their standard of living, and they could talk about what a great guy their father had been without the inconvenience of having to come to Florida twice a year.

The obvious rub was the accidental death clause – the one he had asked about – in the last paragraph of the devil's contract. But so what? He was much likelier to die of something terrible if he didn't take the deal than he was if he did. Besides that, if he took the deal, he'd have at least a few years of life – maybe a whole bunch of years – as a twenty-something. And working for the devil didn't sound so bad. Even if it *was* the dark side, it would have to beat the job he had retired from.

However, there were two other things that caused him concern. First, there was the issue of money. *Young and single would be enough*, he thought. *But young and single, dead broke, and unskilled might not.* He'd push ol' Jake on that one. If it came to it, though, he would probably take the deal without any guarantees of income. He had always been a resourceful guy. Being twenty-something and knowing what he knew now, he would probably do just fine.

The second thing that bothered him was whether he could really trust the devil to honor the deal. *What if he didn't? How could I enforce a contract with the devil? File suit in circuit court? Go to the press? Not likely*, he concluded. He could put all the provisions in the contract he could conceive of, but if the devil didn't honor the contract, there was no recourse. No. If he wanted the deal, he would just have to gamble.

Yep. Noah nodded finally. *I'm gonna do it*. With that, he finished his tea and went to check his will and make sure all his things were in order so Margie could find them. For the first time in a long time, Noah had a decided spring in his step.

Noah Rich wasn't the only one thinking about the deal. Jake was also worried.

The problem for Jake was that the population of leaders in hell was decreasing relative to the population of heaven and the mortal world. The dilemma was similar to that of a world leader. If you were to rule, you just had to have subjects who would do your bidding. Any idiot could declare himself king, head honcho, kahuna, or president, but it was an empty declaration absent quality constituents.

Of course, Jake still had all the old angels that were thrown out of heaven along with him, but there were simply not enough of them to do the business of tempting, corrupting, and generally trying to undermine the so-called good folks. Other than the old angels – he referred to them as his Imperial Guard – Jake had the use of lots of fallen mortals in hell, but they were mostly stupid and inept.

The really evil mortals who could actually carry out a good corruption had to be punished. It was part of Jake's job description. Section 7 clearly said that a major function of hell was "punishing the wicked" who fell under Jake's domain – "The length of punishment to be determined by the Party of the First Part." And some of those punishments went on for... well... ever. That left Jake with the run-of-the-mill dufuses who just couldn't get it together on earth and could absolutely not be relied upon to tempt anyone.

Jake didn't like the deal he'd made, but he didn't have any real choice at the time. To quote one of his subjects whose punishment was getting close to being over, Jake's choice was "to be or not to be." Take the deal or cease to exist... retroactively. Jake was thinking *Where was the choice in that?*

Not only that, but the Black Charter – quite literally a deal with the devil – had what Jake perceived as a *Catch-22* provision, which said "Punishment of the wicked to be carried out exclusively by fallen angels." Considering the number of politicians, terrorists, psychotic dictators, ethnic exterminators, and such, who didn't even get a hearing at the pearly gates on the way to hell, there were barely enough Imperial Guards to keep these quality subdevils from taking over hell and throwing Jake out – much less to help out with recruiting.

In other words, the quality help that Jake needed to handle recruiting was either involved in punishing or being punished for the foreseeable future. What Jake had left were a bunch of ragtag good-for-nothings. If something wasn't done, hell would eventually be overrun by subdevils upsetting everything willy-nilly in their insatiable lust for power, and that would mean the Terminal Provision, Section 666, would kick in. Section 666 provided that "should hell ever cease to fulfill the function envisioned by the Party of the First Part and the Party of the Second Part, it will implode into a black hole and be forever null and void."

As time ticked slowly to a depressing – as far as Jake was concerned – conclusion, Jake decided that if he wanted something done right, he would have to do it himself. So he had personally launched a campaign to recruit mortals. Knowing what happened to the really wicked mortals, his plan was to draft the only slightly wicked but very capable mortals. Noah Rich fell into that category. And the really excellent part of Jake's plan was that, once such a mortal signed his personal contract, there would be no waiting around forever. The act of signing the contract sealed their fate, and in almost no time – in Jake's frame of reference – they could be on the job.

Actually, it wasn't such a bad deal for the mortal. Sure, sooner or later the mortal would get run over by a bus or something. But "sooner or later" – even if it was sooner – could be quite awhile in mortal terms. And if it turned out to be a lot sooner than the mortal had expected, well "you pay your money and take your chances." *I've got to shake the disgusting habit of quoting mortals*, Jake mused.

But pitching the deal was a different thing from closing the deal, and Jake was now concerned that Noah Rich might be having second thoughts. So it was with some trepidation that both Noah and Jake approached the next meeting on Noah's balcony.

Noah knew that Margie would not be home at the hour appointed for his meeting. She would be playing mah-jongg with her girlfriends. In fact, considering the amount of wine consumed at some of Margie's outings, she might not notice that Noah was gone whenever she did return home.

Putting his doubts aside, Noah was caught in a minor quandary. *What did one wear to be transported to youth? Surely I won't be transported naked.* So surveying the beach, he decided on a Tommy Bahama outfit.

Had Jake fully understood Noah's mindset, Noah's garb would have eased his mind immediately about the out-come of today's meeting. However, he didn't, so when Jake arrived, it appeared that Noah might have decided to main-tain his current beach lifestyle.

This time there were no tricks – well, nothing like sit-ting on air. Jake just materialized on the balcony in front of Noah with a minor flash of light and a meager puff of smoke. "Well, Mr. Rich, do we have a deal?"

"I think we can reach an agreement," was Noah's

canny reply.

It did not escape Jake that something remained to be decided. Jake cringed inside, but said "Good. Now I've signed my copy and if you'll just sign yours…"

"Eh, there's a matter that needs to be settled first." Noah had finally decided that the only remaining reasonably foreseeable point was the quality of life issue. "How am I gonna make it wherever I end up?"

Jake almost laughed out loud. The nature of Noah's concern was so minimal, it could hardly be dignified with the word "impediment."

"Noah, ol' buddy…" Jake's informality came from the knowledge that this deal was about to become history. "We'll put you anywhere on earth you want to be, complete with credit cards, ATM account, cash in the bank, and an un-believable set of IDs with whatever name and age you want on it."

Noah thought for a second. *I'm going to do it. This is the best I've felt about anything since I can remember.*

From under his sport coat, Jake produced a pen and gestured for Noah to sign, which Noah did with no reluc-tance.

The deal sealed, a wicked grin crossed Jake's face. "So what's it gonna be, Noah?"

"I was thinking Los Angeles, twenty-five years old, a nice condo in the hills with an ocean view. And like we agreed, I'll need some cash and the other things you mentioned."

"Done," said Jake. "Anything else?"

Noah figured that with a place to live and all the money he would need, he could take care of the rest by himself. "What about our deal?"

"Don't worry about that. You understand the terms. There's no need for me to get involved with your new life until... well, you know when." Jake looked accommodating.

"OK. So what next?"

Jake once again duplicated his levitation thing, floating up and a little off the balcony. "Just give me your hand and we're on our way to your new life."

Noah complied, moving a chair close to the railing so he could step over. But Jake was just a little too far for Noah to take his hand while standing on the chair or the railing. It was going to be necessary to step off. Noah looked at Jake.

Jake nodded confidently.

Noah took the step.

Sure enough Margie Rich had been overserved by the host at her mah-jongg game. She knew she probably shouldn't drive feeling the way she did, but it wasn't far and she would be extra-cautious.

Finally, to the accompaniment of blaring horns, she turned into the basement garage of her condominium. Margie was pleased that she had neither had an accident nor had been stopped for intoxicated driving. So it was quite a shock when she rounded the curve for the second level parking and there, dead ahead, was a police cruiser.

Someone's car must have been broken into, she thought, and tried to ignore the officer who was clearly staring at her as she pulled the big Lincoln almost sideways into her assigned space. Despite the attention of the officer, Margie collected all her things and stepped from her car.

As she began to wobble in the direction of the elevator, she heard, "Ma'am. Hold up there."

Margie froze inside, but turned, gesturing "Who me?"

"Yes, ma'am," the officer replied. "You."

Oh shit, Margie thought. *Now I'm goin' to the big house for sure.*

"Are you Mrs. Margie Rich?" He paused. "The wife of Mr. Noah Rich?"

Margie could absolutely not fathom how the officer knew her name or why Noah might be involved. But she decided someone at the party must have ratted her out and this was some kind of trick question to establish whether she was sober. So she tried to say something sober. "Why is it any of your business?" she replied very slowly and deliberately.

The officer recognized the signs of intoxication, but chose to disregard them under the circumstances. "I'm investigating an accident, and if you're Margie Rich, it concerns you."

Margie thought about that for a moment and decided this officer was going to find out her name one way or the other. "OK, I'm Margie Rich," she said, as if confessing to being Public Enemy Number One.

The officer cleared his throat and seemed to straighten. With a voice exuding sympathy, he said, "Then it's my unfortunate duty to advise you that your husband was killed in a fall from your balcony."

THE LAST CALL

It was one of those days – somewhere in the netherworld between adrenaline-pumping panic and sound asleep. In the last eight hours, I had written ten tickets for seat belt violations, issued a warning for jaywalking, and had a serious talk with a ten-year-old bubblegum thief outside a convenience store. Somehow this wasn't what I had pictured when I signed up to be a police officer.

The good news was my shift was about over and I was heading for the station house. But, like I said, this was one of those days.

"Any unit in the vicinity of Gregory and 9th please respond. Man on the roof of the Crowne Plaza Hotel. See the desk clerk."

This was the same radio that I had presumed dead since my shift began. Now I had maybe thirty minutes to go before heading home and it comes to life. I waited… and waited… and waited some more. Nothing. It's kinda hard to believe I was the only cop in the area at shift change but… you never know.

"Unit 935 responding to Gregory and 9th," I said, taking the call. I could almost hear my comrades laughing as they made their way to the cop shop.

The Crowne Plaza Hotel was a fifteen-story building in downtown Pensacola. At this hour of the day, there wasn't any reason for anyone to be on the roof. Unless the A/C roof unit had gone out, there wasn't anything up there to do. I guess somebody was doing something. My guess was a hotel guest taking in the scenery in violation of the "No Access to Roof" sign.

One of the good things about being a cop is you don't ever have to look for a parking place. I pulled to the main entrance, locked the cruiser in the middle of the drive, and made my way to the front desk.

Of course, all calls are different, but usually there's

some kind of hubbub when you get to the call scene. In this instance, however, the lobby was almost empty. The only sounds were coming from the chatter in the bar. I even had to make a harrumphing noise to get the attention of the guy at the front desk.

"We got a call about somebody on your roof," I said. "What's the problem?"

"Yeah." He squinted his eyes. "A guest coming in said he saw somebody sitting on the ledge on top. Nobody's supposed to be up there. Thought I'd better call the cops… you know? No tellin' what's goin' on up there." He paused. "Probably nothin', but you never know."

It took about ten minutes to ride the elevator to the fifteenth floor, locate the roof exit, and get on top of the building. It was pretty much what you'd expect: gravel on blacktop, big A/C unit in the middle, and an elevated ledge surrounding the whole building. The only thing unusual was the guy sitting with his back to me with his legs crossed, apparently looking out over Pensacola Bay.

Since the Crowne Plaza was one of those modern tall skinny buildings, it only took a couple of steps to be within shouting range. "Hey. What're you doin' up here?" I addressed the guy in my best cop voice.

No response.

Then, about the time I got within grabbing range, the guy shifted his body so he could face me.

"That's far enough, officer," he said in a clear but not hostile voice. He didn't seem to have a weapon. He looked like one of these old duffers who always seem to inhabit golf courses: fit, silver hair, well-tanned smile wrinkles.

I took one more step.

"One more and I'll jump," he said. It didn't sound like a bluff. It was matter-of-fact, like he might be telling me there was a lot of pigeon shit up here.

I stopped and retreated a step.

This was not what I had expected. Like the desk clerk, I figured this was gonna be nothing. At worst, maybe somebody drinking a beer. I was prepared to gruffly escort the perp off the roof and down to the lobby and, after a stern reprimand from the clerk and me, shuffle him out the front door. End of story. Time to go home.

What I seemed to have was a genuine jumper – a suicide. At this very minute, I really, really wished I'd paid more attention in cop school when they were talking about how to handle a potential suicide. Unfortunately, I hadn't. Fortunately, I had my hand radio for backup.

"Could you wait just a second?" I couldn't think of anything else to say as I fumbled for the radio.

"No," he said evenly. "And don't do that. I have no need to talk to anyone, and that includes you." When I didn't put the radio away, he continued. "If you're trying to hurry me along, just keep foolin' with that thing." He nodded at my radio.

I put it away and took another step back. *What does one say in a situation like this*, I wondered. *You don't want to do that? It can't be that bad? Damn that's gonna hurt?* I had no idea. So I said, "You know that's against the law." I wasn't trying to be cute. I just couldn't think of anything else, but it didn't turn out that bad.

The guy looked at me and took a deep breath that seemed to be in preparation for telling me what a dolt I was. Then he stopped and laughed. Not just a chuckle or an ironic snerk, but a real let-it-all-out belly laugh. That, I felt, was good.

When he stopped laughing, I said, "So, you gonna jump?"

He seemed to think about that for a bit, then said, "Yeah, I believe I will." It wasn't as if he'd just made that decision. It was more that the decision had already been made and he was just mentally rechecking it.

Once again: checkmate. If he'd been hysterical or crying or something along those lines, I could have made an effort to console or comfort or introduce reason to him. But he wasn't like that. He gave the impression that he'd thought through all the pros and cons of ending his life and came to a rational decision – at least by his standards.

What can I say to convince him otherwise? I didn't know. What I did know was he was pissing me off. *Why couldn't he off himself on his own time? Why did I have to stick around and clean it up?* So that's what I said.

"Look, dude. You seem to have made up your mind about this, but I'm the guy who's gonna have to clean up the mess. And it's not just a matter of gettin' my hands dirty. I'm talkin' about nightmares, flashbacks, depression – the whole ball of wax."

He looked at me as if to say "Hey! I'm the one dyin' here."

"OK. I understand. This is your deal and I'm just the

hired help. But I think you owe me at least an explanation. I *am* the guy who's gonna have to deal with what's left, you know."

His eyes glazed over as if he were looking inward for an answer. Then he blinked. "OK. Whadaya wanna know?" He paused. "Why, I suppose?"

I nodded.

"OK. But one condition. You stay where you are. Make any move toward me and over I go. When I'm finished, you go back the way you came. Deal?"

"Deal," I said. I knew I wasn't going anywhere one way or the other. Walking off and leaving a suicide sitting on a ledge would get me desk duty before I could say "boo." Cops are notorious liars, but if I could get him talking, maybe I could somehow keep him from jumping.

He took a deep breath and started to say something.

"What's your name?" I interrupted.

He let out the breath. "Not that it matters, but it's John."

"OK." I shrugged.

"What it boils down to…." He stopped. "What's your name?"

"Actually it's John, but I go by Jack."

"Well, Jack, I'm seventy-six years old," he said.

"Lots of people are seventy-six and they don't jump off buildings."

He pursed his lips. "You want the story or not?"

"Sorry," I said, gesturing for him to continue.

He shook his head to get rid of the pique, I suppose. "I wasn't always an old man. I was quite the guy in my time. I could do, and did, just about anything you can think of. Married to a good woman – good looking, smart, athletic. Had a good job making lots of money. Loved to eat good food, drink good whiskey, and have wild sex. Travel? Loved to travel. You name a place and I probably went there. Nice cars. Nice house. Life was pretty much ideal."

"Doesn't seem to fit with jumpin' off a building," I put in. "Wha'd you do to make lots of money?"

"That's the middle of the story. And I was a lawyer, if it matters." He seemed to drift and then refocus. "Then I got older, but things were still pretty good until I hit my late sixties."

"What happened then?" I said.

He let out a sigh and peered off in the distance.

"Time."

I waited.

"First, my wife died. That was the beginning of the end, I guess. Worst thing that ever happened to me. Like losing part of myself." He paused again. "You married?"

"Yeah. Two kids," I said.

"You love her?"

I thought that was a bit personal, but answered anyway. "Yeah. She's a good woman."

At that point, he began to drift again and I thought seriously about making a grab for him, but he seemed to sense my intention and snapped back to the present. He gave me a knowing smile. I shrugged.

"It took me awhile after her death, but I began to rejoin the living, and things seemed to be getting better – if you call hanging out with the local geriatric mafia getting better." His chuckle turned into a sigh. "But then my health started to go."

"That happens to everybody sooner or later. Some people don't have the opportunity to get old."

"Ha." This was not a good "ha." "You say that like you've been there... and you haven't. What are you, thirty-something?"

"Well, close." My answer sounded kinda weak even to me.

"I remember when I was thirty-something. I heard about older people's health going, and I guess I figured that meant they got more colds or something. But that's not how it works. It starts slow, but it's just one thing after another. You can't see. You can't hear. You can't play. Food's not so good. Even good whiskey doesn't do it for you. And that's the good part. That's if you don't get some horrible disease like cancer, heart problems, diabetes, and on and on." He paused in thought. "Until finally there's nothing to look forward to."

I started to say something, but he cut me off.

"Do you know what it means to have nothing to look forward to?"

I wasn't sure I did, but I figured he'd tell me. And he did.

"In life, no matter how bleak things get, there's always something good that could possibly happen. Somebody dies and leaves you millions. A beautiful woman picks you up in a bar. You get well. Something, right?"

"Those are things that could still happen to you," I suggested.

"Ha." This "ha" wasn't quite so bitter. "That's not the point. And you're right. Those things could conceivably happen to me. But the point is: if all those things happened to me tomorrow, it would be meaningless. Because when your health goes, there's nothing you can do with them. Without your health, you can't enjoy them. Life is a two-parter. First, you have to have things. Second, you have to be able to enjoy having them. If you don't have both parts, you got squat." He let that sink in. "And that's what I got... squat."

I hadn't ever thought of that. I guess you don't at thirty-something. The second part of the equation is always a given. The first part is the hard part when you're younger. But if he was right, he had a point. What could I say? When the book of life ceases to be of interest, maybe it *is* time to turn the last page.

He must have sensed the wheels turning. "So, whadaya say, Jack? Time to let me take care of business?"

From nowhere I can think of but sophomore English, I said, "Go not gently into that good night. Rage against the fading of the light." I said it in the tone of an order combined with a plea.

Indeed, that was a funny thing for a cop to say – very uncoply. And it apparently surprised him as much as me. For the longest time he seemed to ponder the meaning and implications.

If this was the deciding point, my money was still on the abyss. And I couldn't really just walk off and let him die. Tilting slightly in his direction and coiling my legs to spring, I said, "But listen," and gesticulated as a distraction. Then I dove to him like a swimmer coming off the platform.

I wasn't a swimmer, but I did manage to catch him around the waist as he leaned toward empty space. If my adrenaline flow hadn't been on max, this little maneuver would have really hurt. I got hold of him just as I slammed into the ledge where he was seated.

It took some time, but wrestling a frail old man back over the edge of death wasn't all that challenging. However, after hitting the ledge, I didn't just jump right up and cuff him. For a while, we lay side by side – me panting like a locomotive.

"You know what, Jack?" he asked. Being dragged over a ledge hadn't winded him at all. "You're right about that 'go not gently' stuff. But tell me. Does 'rage against the fading of the light' mean continuing to struggle with forces beyond your control? Or does it mean taking the situation in hand and thus giving death the ol' middle digit on the way out your exit of choice?"

Hey, I'm a cop. I don't get paid to parse poetry. And besides that, it wasn't a quick-answer question. I did my job and bundled John off to the psych unit at one of the local hospitals. I would probably give the question more consideration later – probably much later.

Once the mental health professionals did what they do, John would be released. In my opinion, John wasn't crazy; maybe just a little depressed for good reason. But the shrinks would give him meds and perhaps a little jolt of electricity. At some point, John would tell them he had seen the light, and that would be that. At least, that would be that as far as the system was concerned. We had all done our jobs just like we were supposed to.

However, my money was on our seeing John again. I didn't think John would see us, though – unless he was looking down from the afterlife and laughing at our attempts to forestall the inevitable. But that's how we humans do things. We believe that even if it doesn't work, we need to do something. It makes us feel better.

KICKING THE BUCKET

As the Arizona sun beat down mercilessly, an intrepid posse of canyoneers (let's call 'em the IPC for short) struggled through mule doodoo, odd-angled boulders, and crossties.

"Crossties? What are crossties?" you ask.

Crossties are those things between railroad tracks. They're also placed on hiking trails by Satan to test your will to live.

Roughly four hours earlier, this same group had been tucked away fast asleep (kinda) in their beds. Shortly before God himself arose, the IPC launched from their racks, staggered to the communal café, gobbled down breakfast, and after a brief but not highly effective toilette, regrouped with full packs and began to trudge toward heaven – or somewhere very close to it.

Two hours ago, the ascent had been halted for a hearty feast of one small bagel, a small bag of pretzels, and something that looked like a large dog turd. Presumably, this mysterious diet would fuel the final ascent to the top.

"So whadaya sayin', your scout troop went for a hike?" you query. "So big deal."

"Big deal, eh? What if I told you that the IPC were financially comfortable adults?"

"So the guys went for a little adventure?"

"What if I told you this was a mixed gender group?"

"Tough chicks. So?"

"What if I told you the age of the group ranged from sixty to mid-seventy, and skewed to the upper end?"

"A bunch of lost Alzheimer patients? Chuckle."

"'Chuckle' yourself. What if I added that the IPC suffered from a variety of maladies – from hip replacements to heart conditions to torn muscles to healing leg breaks to blisters – that would keep your normal healthy twenty-something securely at home in bed? And we probably didn't hear all of it. Like talking about how much money you have when you're in Aspen – someone's always got more. So with the IPC, bringing up a sore toe would just be embarrassing."

"Then, aside from the sanity issue, I'd have to ask why."

Well, as most such fanciful adventures start, this one began several months earlier in the rosy glow of good wine. As the matter of life experiences was broached, one group member had proclaimed, "I've never hiked the Grand Canyon. That'd be on my bucket list." Another had never even seen it. And, as these things go, one thought led to another. The end result was someone volunteered to arrange such a hike.

"It won't be too tough," she said.

"We can stay at Phantom Ranch at the bottom and hike out after a day of rest," she said.

"All we need to do is train a little. Hiking the canyon is the most awesome experience of a lifetime," she said.

Leaving unsaid: "You wouldn't want to 'cash out' without doing it… unless you're already too old." Nothing was mentioned at that point about blazing sun, mule doodoo, and crossties. No one even thought about bunk beds, limited johns, six hours down, eight hours up, and a nice five-hour hike on the "day of rest" in between.

Plans were made, e-mails flew, and, since the actual departure time was in the distant future, excitement soared as money changed hands to lock-in a spot on the big trip.

I've taken a little poetic license with the reasons just advanced to make it comprehensible why twenty or so "golden agers" – if you can stomach that euphemism – would come out of pleasant surroundings and tromp up and down a trail only fit for mules and wild-eyed young outdoorsmen. I wasn't actually there at the inception, and I'd rather not insult the IPC. My story is a bit different and a lot more difficult to understand. However, I'm not worried about insulting myself.

My personal adventure started when the agent provocateur called and said something like, "Hey, a bunch of us are gonna hike the Grand Canyon. Wanna come with?"

My first thought was *Wanna come with what... or who?* But after deciding that the absence of the direct object of a preposition in a sentence was just a quaint midwestern expression, I said "Been there, done that, but first let me talk to my reason-for-living." The caller understood. He was married.

My reason-for-living and I had both hiked the canyon twenty years prior – down three hours and up six hours all in one day. The next day we were doing a first class rendition of "the canyon shuffle." We allowed as how it would have been a lot more fun (sane?) if we'd stayed the night at the bottom and could now walk like human beings.

The urge to recapture lost youth and vigor? The canyon grandeur we recalled? The need to do things undone? Maybe it was the wine after all. Whatever. We signed on.

In no time at all, we were blanketed with brochures and e-mails from the outfitter: Road Scholars – An Elder Hostel. (Somehow that last part was not consonant with any kind of youth – lost or otherwise.) In addition to the information that absolutely had nothing to do with the Grand Canyon hike (such as hiking the Mall of America), there were at least a million pages of questions challenging our ability to actually walk. Not to mention lots of curious advice about preparation – "Trim your toenails."

Some of the advice had to do with odds and ends we might need on the hike: walking sticks, a bandanna, a flashlight, earplugs, a day-and-a-half pack, a three-liter water container. *Why,* I thought, *do I need walking sticks? I can walk just fine. And a bandanna, earplugs, and a flashlight? Are we gonna blow a bank vault at night?*

My wife and I already had backpacks, rucksacks, and one-liter bladders for water, but not day-and-a-half packs or three-liter bladders. So it was off to REI for some things that we'd probably use once. In retrospect, all those things were necessary. So I'm glad we obediently followed directions. (Clue: Bandannas are for sweat. Flashlights are for late night trips to the potty. Earplugs are for people who didn't get tired enough to sleep through a bit of snoring.)

As the day of departure approached, we began to have second thoughts, but by that time we had invested way too much in gear and training. We were going whether we liked it or not.

The plan was that we should all meet at the mighty Maswik Lodge the day before the festivities began so our guide (Jeff) could tell us necessary stuff and give us snacks. (I'd like to add here that, as a snack provider, Jeff was awesome. I actually gained weight on the hike.)

The Maswik Lodge was likely built by Fred Harvey or

Geronimo – I know for sure that it was there twenty years ago when I first hiked the canyon. It has not changed one iota. Prominent in my twenty-year-old recollection, and to this very day, the Maswik has no air conditioning. Perhaps the reasoning is that if you can't spend a night without A/C, you sure can't hike the Grand Canyon. Personally, I think that reasoning is fatally flawed. There's lots of things I can't do, but I still want air conditioning. But I don't want to quibble. There was no A/C. I survived. I'll never go back to the Maswik again. On the other hand, in twenty more years, I probably won't remember I was ever at the Maswik. So... who knows?

In any case, Day One of the bold adventure consisted of a "practice hike." Practice hike? Why would we need a practice hike? If anyone hadn't practiced by the time we got to the Grand Canyon, it would be a little late to start.

But there it was: one hour down and back up in full gear following our fearless leader Jeff. The trip down was very regimented and education oriented. At the turn-around point, Jeff let us go. Off we raced to the top like wild animals sprung from cages... kinda. At the top, we dispersed. Some of us saw this as a wonderful opportunity to find out if the

"Pizza Pub" at the Maswik Lodge really had beer.

Thinking back, I'm guessing that the practice hike served one of two purposes – maybe both. One would be to fill time. That way the Grand Canyon hike could be billed as a five-day adventure, if you count dinner the first night, instead of four. Number two would be to weed out the unfit, the idea being that if a person couldn't make it through the practice hike, he/she sure couldn't make it down and back up the canyon. However, I would have been decidedly unhappy if, after training, buying gear, and making my way to the canyon rim (not to mention being subjected to the Maswik), somebody said I couldn't go.

For whatever reason, it didn't weed out any of the IPC. Those folks were tough as old boots. I think some of them even went off hiking after the practice hike.

The Descent

The day before the "big day," by request Jeff allowed as how we might be able to start the hike at some reasonable hour, like eight or nine o'clock in the morning. After all, it really wasn't hot and the trip down only took around six hours at most. Most of the IPC thought that was a reasonable course of action. Some of our group had only heard rumors about the existence of eight o'clock in the morning.

Then we met guide number two – Jen. Jen was a former park ranger and a very nice person. But the Rules of the Wilderness were the rules of the wilderness. One of those rules apparently is "One must start very early for anything one might do in the wilderness." Reason aside, rules is rules. We assembled at six-fifty in front of the Maswik to ride the park bus to the rim for a seven o'clock start.

(I would also learn that early rising is not the only Rule of the Wilderness. Another one is "Don't throw rocks." I suppose if everyone threw a rock off a Grand Canyon trail, sooner or later all the rocks would end up in the bottom. Who knows? Jen said "Don't".)

I'm gonna skip over a description of the Grand Canyon. Not because it's not important. It is. The problem here is that I don't have command of enough superlatives to adequately describe it. Truly, though, the Grand Canyon is an awe-inspiring, almost mystically religious place. The descent from the south rim is like stepping into a beautiful portrait and moving back in time. I'm sure most of the IPC felt the same sense of awe winding down the steep trail.

Unfortunately, with every silver lining comes a cloud. The South Kaibab Trail (that's pronounced *ky-bab*, not kabob like the food; apparently, only fools and tenderfoots make that mistake) is a very steep trail. At many points, there's a cliff face on one side and nothing on the other. Well, not really nothing. There is something on the other side: a sheer drop of maybe a mile or two. One false stumble and only the lizards and rattlesnakes would keep company with what would be left of your battered corpse.

You see the problem? Imagine the scenery-dazzled IPC with cameras, working diligently to capture the majesty in person and digitally, while simultaneously struggling mightily to avoid the drop into the abyss. They say top NFL quarterbacks can actually sense the presence of a defensive rusher. I'm not sure the IPC could feel the fatal tipping point of the trail.

Here's where Jen and Jeff earned their money. Like sheep dogs nipping the heels of wayward lambs, they were here, there, and everywhere reminding the IPC that a picture may be worth a thousand words, but that just doesn't work out if the camera goes over the cliff with you. We had lots of photo breaks. (Perhaps that's why Ranger Jen made us start early.)

Did I mention that the South Kaibab was very steep? So not a lot of folks used it? So there's only one real toilet facility on the whole trail? Maybe that's why we stopped for our lunch break at the only ugly place in the entire Grand Canyon. It had a "gravity toilet." It also had great big ants and little biddy wiggly rocks for dining room chairs. Lunch was pretty quick.

Before we get to the bottom, I want to mention something else. Among the many fascinating things he told us, Jeff explained why a hiker gets leg fatigue and soreness, as well as how to avoid it. The "why" had to do with white blood cells draining from the entire body and being lodged in the feet. Or maybe it was the red blood cells in the legs. Or maybe it was the other way around. I don't know. But at the time, it sounded like a pretty good explanation and it beat saying something like "your legs just get tired if you walk too long."

Anyway, to combat leg fatigue and soreness, it's necessary to drain whatever it is back to where it should be and out of the legs… or feet. Rather than undergoing a complicated medical procedure right there on the trail, what Jeff prescribed was to periodically lie on your back holding your feet and legs up in the air. Gravity would then put everything back where it was supposed to be. Neat, eh?

I didn't try it. I never could find a comfortable looking rock that would accommodate my fat body. That, and disengaging my backpack, getting down on the ground, and then getting back up was just too much effort.

"The point?" you ask. "Get to the point."

The point is: many of the IPC did try Jeff's remedy. Imagine a group of fifteen or so senior types lying on their backs along a hiking trail with their legs in the air. Now imagine how a dead cockroach looks. Now imagine an uninitiated hiker stumbling on this scene. Chortle. Chortle.

Anyway, after many crossties, one of the startling beauties of the Grand Canyon became manifest – the emerald-green Colorado River cutting through the ancient rugged canyon cliffs. To get the idea, you could use Google Earth at a max magnification, but you'd have to also imagine being able to walk into your computer screen. Wow!

And down and down.

Finally, we crossed the Colorado on a suspension bridge, made a hard left, a hard right, and there was Phantom

Ranch about a quarter-mile up a gently slanting trail.

El Rancho Fantasma

Welcome to Camp Cedarbrook.

More than sixty years ago, I went to summer camp. It was a place that couldn't have been too far out of Dallas, but then, who knows how a five-year-old perceives time in a car? Whatever its Texas location, someone had stolen it, moved it to the bottom of the Grand Canyon, and renamed it. There were the cabins, bunk beds, communal dining hall, and communal bathrooms and showers. There was even an irrigation ditch right outside our cabin. *Déjà vu* all over again.

There was, however, one highly significant difference between Camp Cedarbrook and Phantom Ranch. Phantom Ranch sold cold beer in the communal dining hall. And after the hike down, that one fact made up for any problems I may have had with the accommodations – at least for the time being.

Good ol' Jeff had prepared us for the bunk beds with ten relative strangers in a cabin. So I wasn't surprised. Being a gentleman, I offered my reason-for-living the top bunk. Some might not agree with my interpretation, but I reasoned that, at my weight, there could be a tragic accident if the top bunk would not support me. Besides that, Reason-For-Living is younger than I am. Hey, in summer camp, the top was always the bunk of choice.

But top or bottom wasn't really the problem. It was how the bed was constructed *vis-à-vis* the mattress size. The mattress was plenty soft. It just didn't make it to the edge of the bed sideboards. So sitting on the edge or climbing into or out of the bed was a problem. Of course, a person could butt-balance on the side plank if that person had buns of steel. Otherwise, it was in or out. And climbing in or out of bed was akin to mounting a horse: throw that leg over, and swing on up. By the time we hiked out, those of us who never succeeded in mastering the bed-mounting technique looked like we had been beaten severely about the back thigh and front shin.

For those of you who might be thinking *You're just a bitcher and a malcontent*, that's not entirely true. I see myself more as an op-ed journalist: my job is to find fault where there is none, then exploit it. Besides that, Camp Ce... er, Phantom Ranch had some pretty good points. Breakfast and dinner were excellent. The ranch workers were friendly. The beer was good and cold.

But the best part was the bedtime story that Jeff and Jen read to us each night. Really. I mean, when was the last time anyone read you a bedtime story? Actually, I don't think anyone ever read me a bedtime story, but that's beside the point. It was nice – except maybe the one about scorpions.

Did I mention the excitement of grappling from my bunk, creeping through the cabin with my flashlight, and trying to tinkle in the middle of a deadly silent night surrounded by ten relative strangers who were probably listening? Or the smoke alarm in the cabin that, for no apparent reason, went off in the middle of the night – both nights? No? OK. Never mind.

The Ascent

Once again the Rules of the Wilderness came into play with a vengeance. Breakfast at five o'clock... *in the morning*. Unless I just leaped from my bunk and ran scraggly into the communal dining room, that translated into a four-thirty wakeup time. I'm not sure I've seen four-thirty in the morning since I was in college – and then it was from the other side. But I now knew that rules is rules, and if I didn't do it,

I'd be scaling the cliffs on an empty stomach.

At some point or another that morning, after our six o'clock start, I finally woke up. I think it was when we turned off the river trail and started up... and up... and up. This time we were on Bright Angel Trail.

You remember the problem I explained about the view during the descent? Well, this was different. Somewhere along the way, I ceased to care if there was a view or a bottomless chasm on one side. However, the view became important – stopping to look at it was an excellent excuse to just stop... and breathe.

Once we got in our stride – step, step, drag yourself over the crosstie, suck up water, suck up water – Reason-For-Living and I were on a roll. Maybe we could do this.

But what's happening? Jeff and Jen are telling us to stop. *Stop!?! Please don't make us stop. I'll never get started again.*

To their credit, I suppose Jeff and Jen felt responsible for us. Even though Bright Angel is a single trail which even a blind old person could follow, who can say what an aging warrior might do? Maybe jump off the side. Stop to pee on the trail. Start throwing rocks.

We stopped. And then, absent any kind of rhythmic

delusions that we might actually make it to the top, we started again.

I'm not sure what time it was, but eventually we ate lunch at a wide spot on the trail called Indian Gardens – an oasis in the canyon walls. Forewarned is forearmed. I had stolen some bacon at breakfast. I felt like Oliver Twist, but I didn't care. The sack lunch from Phantom Ranch wouldn't cut it. Besides that, I think Jen had stolen part of a steak last night at dinner. I kept eyeing her, but she wasn't sharing.

And that's it. I could tell you more about the ascent, but it wouldn't be very interesting. Step, step, drag yourself over a crosstie, suck water, suck water, *etcetera, etcetera, ad nauseam.*

Finally, though, we saw the tunnel through the cliff. It was maybe a half-mile from the rim, but it had curious and miraculous powers. We would make it to the rim. We could stop walking soon. There would be cold beer at the top. This wasn't so hard after all.

"So," you say. "It was a horrible trip?"

I didn't say that. It was a great trip. A fantastic experience. We met some people we really liked who were absolutely inspiring.

"Eh… that's not how it sounded," you say. "Would you do it again?"

Well… maybe not tomorrow, but next year? Who knows?

"What about all the bad stuff?" you say.

It wasn't bad. Perhaps a little challenging. But sometimes it's good to be pushed out of your comfort zone. Besides that, as an ancient curmudgeonly philosopher once said, "Half the fun of doing anything is bitching about it."

LIBERATION FANTASY

Back in the dim mists of time, I graduated from college and immediately went to work. There was no backpacking through Europe. There was no period of self-discovery. There was no money. But there was a government that wanted to be repaid all the funds I was lucky enough to have borrowed to pay most of my college expenses. Oddly enough, through the lens of present day, I felt obligated to pay it all back.

So for the next forty years, it was me and the company. If I did whatever the company asked for eight to ten hours a day for five or six days a week, like a fine clock, every two weeks, bingo, my paycheck materialized on my desk.

At first, of course, it was a shock. I knew I had signed

on for whatever the going rate was back then for college graduates, but when the paycheck came it was seriously less than that. The company wasn't stealing from me. They had made a commitment and, by golly, they stuck to it. It was the government – that same government that I regularly made payments to for my college loan – that was causing my check, which should have been X, to be X minus a bunch. They were taking out money just so I'd be able to pay my taxes come April. And so I could retire with some money at some point so distant in the future, I couldn't even conceive of it.

Neither of these reasons for my light check seemed fair. I recognized that it was my responsibility to pay my taxes and to save money for retirement. But what the government said was that this withholding of my money was necessary; otherwise irresponsible people would not pay their taxes or save for their retirement. Then the great and benevolent government would have to take care of them – either in prison or an old folks home. I would later understand that those reasons were only a very small part of the truth. These payroll deductions were merely a way to tax me more, so the government could do other things with my money until it was time to dribble out a meager retirement payment.

No matter, though – it's our way in this country. At some point, I married, had children, and did all the things social parents do. What I mean by that is, when I wasn't working for the company, I coached my kids in about all the sports a kid can play, went to countless recitals, did scouts, attended gazillions of skill demonstrations, graduations, and entertained – and was entertained by – friends, other kids' parents, and business associates. On Sundays, I would have rested because of the pace of the preceding week plus the Saturday yard ordeal, but Sundays were for church and visits to parents and in-laws.

This frenzied existence began when the first kid blessed us with his presence, and never let up until the youngest one slammed the door on her way to college. At that point, my life merely changed – as opposed to becoming calmer – because with three kids in various stages of education at unreasonably priced schools, it became necessary to work more. My wife even got a job. She told her friends that, with the kids gone, she needed something to do. That, of course, wasn't it at all.

Sometime in my mid-fifties, my last little princess got tired of being educated and went to work. I was, at last, free of the burden. At least, that's what I thought. I had managed to "pay as I went." So my wife and I could slow down a bit. *Ah, yes*, I thought. *Time to reap the fruits of my labor.*

That's when the death cycle started. I call it that because heretofore things were becoming and growing. Now life had plateaued for a while – a very brief while – and then people started declining, winding-up, dying.

With four aging parents and no useful siblings, it fell to my wife and I to care for our moms and dads as they slowly faded to nothing. Obviously they wouldn't all just give up the ghost at the same time. Not only did they each take their time, but they also did it on nonconcurrent calendars, as if they were taking turns hopping on that last downward slide.

So now, instead of being totally occupied with the lives of our children, we became totally occupied with the lives of our parents – when the company didn't beckon, of course. This was the time of wills, doctors, hospitals, late night calls, nursing homes, and exchanging roles. This was the grimmest phase yet.

My dad hung on the longest, but one day he just closed his eyes without so much as a "see you later" and died. With his passing, I once again moved to a new, more sane existence.

And that's when the company decided it was time for us to go our separate ways. They didn't fire me. I just hit that magic age and it was time to retire.

It was really kind of sad and certainly odd. We, the company and I, had been together for forty years. Five or six days a week, before the sun came up, except maybe on the summer solstice, I would rise from bed, groom myself, go to the company, and stay there until after dark. I spent way more of my conscious hours with the company than anyone or anything else in my life.

My leaving was not cause for a gold watch or a farewell celebration. The company didn't do that sort of thing. But that was just fine with me because what they did do was guarantee that as long as I lived, or my wife lived, they would continue to send a check every two weeks. With payback for all those taxes I had given to the government, this would maintain my standard of living as it was when I retired.

In fact, for maybe the preceding ten years, I had fantasized about retirement. With no familial or serious monetary obligations, I would have all the time I wanted to do whatever struck me – or I could do nothing at all. I would be liberated from responsibility. So it was with a big grin and a spring in my step that I left the company, never to return.

At first, the options were too daunting. Imagine being a bird living in a very nice cage most of your life. Then someone opens the cage door and says "It's all yours. Enjoy it." I suspect many birds accidentally freed soon die. They have no idea what to do or how to deal with freedom. Fortunately, I wasn't a bird. I had some preconceived ideas about things I might do. It just took awhile to sort them out.

While doing that, I became reacquainted with golf. I began an exercise program with light weights and some reasonably serious biking. Some days I just wandered around and looked at things. Oddly, due to my erroneous preconception of older people, I began to feel physically better, healthier. I was getting ready to embrace that part of life I had missed. My wife was a little surprised at the increase in amorous impulses. Perhaps for that reason, she developed her own physical health program. Life was good.

Of course, it doesn't work this way for everybody. This period can be very hard on a married couple. For forty-odd years, the beautiful bride and handsome groom have been Mom and Dad. In that parental time period and mindset, they have forgotten what attracted them to one another in the first place. They have devolved into a ricochet relationship. The line of the relationship doesn't move directly from husband to wife; it's reflected from husband by some third party – like kids – to wife. Or vice versa. Absent that intervening third party, they don't have a relationship. And this might have been the case for my wife and I, but by the time I retired, the kids had been functionally gone for ten or fifteen years. We had adjusted and were quite comfortable with each other. We took a blood oath not to refer to each other as "Mom" or "Dad."

It was as my wife and I sat planning our great world tour that the call came. Perhaps it wasn't then at all. Maybe it just seems like it came then.

"Hello," I said.

"Dad," the familiar voice of my middle son responded. "I've got a problem."

It turned out that he had lost his job, could no longer afford his apartment, and needed a place to live temporarily.

I wanted to explain to him that his mom and I were now a happy twosome with no ambitions of expanding our family unit. His old room was now his mother's sewing suite.

And, in fact, we were about to hit the road for adventure wherever it led. But what I said was "It's just fine for you to live with us while you get back on your feet. When are you coming?"

"Tomorrow," he said.

"See you when you get here," I managed to say in an affectionate voice. What I wondered was just what he had been doing from the time he knew of his situation until now. It occurred to me that this seat-of-the-pants flying might have something to do with why he was now unemployed. But what's a parent to do? Explain that there's a nice homeless shelter downtown that will provide a cot and one meal a day?

When I advised my wife, she sat silently for a while before she answered. "Well, if we're going to be gone for a month or two, we need someone to check on our house anyway. This will work out fine."

Right, I thought, but didn't say. I was thinking about the movie *Risky Business* and young Tom Cruise and what happens when parents leave their kid at home alone. Now we were three… again.

For the first week of our reunion, I found myself carefully watching my son for signs of maturity, or the lack thereof. From the way he applied himself to his job search, I was beginning to think that our world tour might work out after all. It was then that the phone intervened yet a second time.

"Hello," I said.

"Dad, this is your daughter," as if I wouldn't know.

"Yes, dear. I know."

"Do you remember Tommy Farrell?"

"Is he the one who rode the motorcycle?"

"No. That was Wild Thing."

"Then, no. I don't remember Tommy Farrell."

"Well…" She paused. "Tommy and I are getting married."

"Well…" I paused. "Congratulations. Does your mother know?"

"No."

"Oh." I paused again. "When is the big day?"

"As soon as possible."

With more questions and some prodding, she explained that she and Tommy were in love and had "kinda" been living together, but they had planned to postpone marriage for a while. Unfortunately, the law of nature had taken its normal and natural course and, within pretty close to nine months, I would be a grandfather. Since they had planned marriage at some point, they believed it would be good to do it right away under the circumstances.

I had to agree that, her premises accepted, a wedding was probably a good idea. I assumed the ceremony would be something quiet and quick with a nice justice of the peace.

"Let me talk to mom," she said.

After giving the phone to my wife, from the next room I heard tears, hysterics, and some agreeing coos. Then the phone call ended and my wife announced, "She wants a big wedding in our church next month."

Now it was my turn for hysterics, but no tears or agreeing coos. Visions of ships sailing and dollars flying from my billfold engulfed my consciousness. However, after calming down, I conceded that my daughter's proposed course would be possible. I did not agree that it was the best way or that I was happy about it, but with my wife and daughter firmly aligned against me, it looked like one big wedding coming up; one world tour going down.

After sitting and ruminating for a while, I walked to the telephone and dialed my first son. My wife watched as if surveying a potential homicidal maniac.

"Hello," he answered.

"When are you coming?" I said.

"When am I coming where, Dad?" He recognized me.

"Home, of course. Or maybe you're a little short of money and need a loan?"

"Dad? Are you OK?"

"Well, your brother has moved back home. Your sister is knocked-up and demanding a big wedding very soon. I figured why wait around for the last shoe to drop. You must need something."

He laughed. I didn't. My wife intervened. "Stop that. He's gonna think you're crazy," she said, as she grabbed the phone.

The following chat established that Son One did, in fact, not need anything, and that I was just a little upset – as opposed to straight-running nuts. Things were set right. Time marched on.

The wedding turned out all right. My suggestion about a nice JP with my wife and I as witnesses had resulted in my wife threatening celibacy. So I sprang for the cash, gave my little princess away, and grinned like I was really happy to have gained yet another son.

At some point after the wedding but before the arrival of my granddaughter, Son Two found a job. Not long after that, he moved back to his own apartment. It seemed that he was about as happy living with us as we were having him live with us. Our points of dissatisfaction weren't exactly the same. Ours had to do with freedom from responsibility and time with each other. His related more to the odds of getting laid at mom and dad's house. In a way, I guess the points were similar. We didn't discuss it and parted amicably.

Now, I assumed, was our window of opportunity. Both sons were up and running, and our daughter was some other guy's problem. This was just another illustration of how little men know of women – even after forty or fifty years of marriage.

"When do we leave?" I said, as Son Two closed the front door.

"Leave?" said my wife, as if I had just suggested a threesome.

"Yeah. You know. World tour. Big adventure." I was mystified.

"Darling, we have a pregnant daughter. She's gonna need a lot of help from her mother."

At this point, I believe what was left of my life flashed before my eyes. There would be no hiking through Switzerland, biking through Denmark, chasing kangaroo through Australia. By the time we had another window of opportunity, wherever we went would be on a bus with a bunch of old people.

As it turned out, I was right, but it really wasn't all that bad. I threw myself into that great game of golf. After a while, Sons One and Two married and had children. I was awash with tiny people who called me PawPaw. When she could tear herself away from midwifing and babysitting, my wife and I did take some short trips alone and enjoyed them. Later we went by bus, which wasn't all that bad, either.

One day on the golf course, for no apparent reason, I had a heart attack. And as the light faded and that good night encroached, I wondered just what kind of responsibilities I was in for now.

NO COUNTRY FOR OLD WUSSES

Roughly six months after my wife of thirty years walked out the door and took up with my doctor, I retired. I say "retired" instead of "quit" because I'm close to that age and it sounds better. Quitting implies giving up on something, whereas retiring has a certain grace – the idea that you've done all you could and withdrawn with dignity. But the fact of the matter is that it was just an OK job and, absent someone to support other than me, it wasn't worth the time. Especially considering that I don't really have all that much time left.

The wife? Well, she was probably right when she said that we were just sharing space; no profound attachment. And I don't know how that started. We never had kids because just the two of us seemed to be enough. Then somehow we grew apart.

My passion, other than work and her, was sports: playing sports, watching sports, reading about sports. I was a fan and a jock wannabe. She, on the other hand, was a gardener: flowers, grass, plants, anything she could grow. We both tried to become involved in each other's avocation, but she hated sports as much as I hated gardening. In fact, I think we came to believe that anyone who would participate in the other's hobby was a dolt.

I guess the split started when we agreed to disagree. In the end, we didn't have much of anything in common other than occasional sex.

But still. My doctor? I mean, I'd been seeing him since before I met her. At some point in the marriage, she began seeing him as well. (That's "seeing" as in seeking medical treatment, as opposed to "seeing" as in banging him on a regular basis.) Apparently things progressed. Honestly, I felt more betrayed by my doctor's behavior than my wife's. Surely there's something in the Hippocratic oath about not boinking your patient's wife. Maybe the concept gets muddled when the patient's wife is also a patient. Who knows? The whole thing pissed me off. But on the other hand, even a sports nut needs a little romance in his life. So in the end, the split was probably the best thing. I just wish she hadn't stolen my doctor.

In any case, if there's any such thing as an amicable divorce, ours was one. We each kept our cars and personal items, sold everything else, and split the cash. She even paid her own lawyer.

Like I said, after about six months – the time from her announcement to the final decree – I just didn't see the point, not counting the income, of spending all my time doing something I really didn't care that much about. So almost on impulse, one day I walked into my boss's office, gave him thirty days notice, and thirty days later I was gone.

Of course, it wasn't like I just quit with no thought of what I might do afterwards. Running off to a Caribbean island struck me as stupid. Sure it would be cool to hang around on the beach drinking umbrella drinks and chasing tourist chicks. At least it would be neat for a while, but then what? At my age, too much hangin' and drinkin' would certainly shorten whatever time I had left. Besides that, I am not your basic buff-bronzed beach type. I'm an old... well, oldish man. The mental image of a crazy old street person hitting on sweet young things just didn't work.

However, the mountains of Colorado sounded good. We – the philandering, doctor-stealing bitch and I – had vacationed often in Vail in both summer and winter. I had always enjoyed it – biking, hiking, skiing, snowshoeing. And there were lots of kindred spirits and pretty people.

I had no illusions about working as a ski instructor or river guide, burning the candle at both ends. What I had in mind was something like a kinder gentler ski bum. Instead of four guys in a trailer way down valley, maybe a nice one-bedroom apartment in town and within easy reach of the ski slope – something with a view and a wood-burning fireplace for the cold snowy winter nights. Rather than three jobs to make ends meet, perhaps something in the hotel or condominium business – a front-desk person or a concierge – having enough time off to pursue the mountain sports and an occasional mature female.

I had enough money to last for a few years without working, if I didn't go wild. Plus, getting some kind of part-time job would be a good social entrée. So I gave all my former working clothes to the Salvation Army, packed what was left in my car, and hit the road for Vail.

I would later come to understand that there are three groups of people who live in a ski resort like Vail: the wealthy, the workers, and a middle class that has figured out how to make enough money to live in, or close to, the resort. The wealthy are mostly part-time second-home owners. The workers are either Hispanics or they are youngsters who have dropped out of the real world for a while. The middle class is mostly professionals, successful trades people, and real estate agents. Except during late fall when there's nothing to do because there's no snow yet, and spring when the snow melts and it's too muddy, the tourists form a kind of overlay on that semi-stable triad. Even the permanent three tend to be gone in the shoulder seasons because, aside from the lack of recreation, there's no one around to whom they can sell stuff. Astonishingly, even some real estate agents vanish. Since I wasn't any of those things, I was something of a misfit. Not a good omen, but I didn't know that at the time.

My personal odyssey began in late spring. So there was nobody home. Or at least there weren't many people home. The hotels and big condominiums stay open with a skeleton crew. For me this was a good news/bad news situation. The good news was the rent was cheap by resort standards. The bad news was that all the affordable rentals were short term.

Other than the wealthy, people tend to come and go in the Vail Valley. They come and in fairly short order – one season – discover that they can't make enough money to live there. Or they burn out working, skiing, and partying every day. Or they have a vision of being a forty-something ski bum with no future and nothing but Social Security and a MacJob to live on when they hit sixty-five.

Once again, being a newby, I only saw the number of vacated apartments from which I could choose and an opportunity to get a jump on the part-time job competition. Besides, I wasn't looking for negatives. I was looking for excitement.

After surveying the available places to rent, I got my first reality shot. There would be no wood-burning fireplace, and the only view I would likely get was the back of some other apartment – with luck, a tree. I also realized that, before I committed to anything, I'd better find out what sort of job I could get, or my savings would be only a memory after a year.

The resort company was a good outfit to work for, but the jobs they had available were seasonal or full-time. That meant I'd have a job when I wanted to play or wouldn't have a job when there was nothing else to do. The next best offer was working as the relief desk clerk for a large hotel. Sounded perfect. However, it being the shoulder season, they didn't really need anyone until around mid-June. That was over a month away.

On the other hand, Burger Biggie needed an "assistant manager trainee" right now. So I snapped up both jobs thinking I'd part company with Burger Biggie when the hotel needed me. I didn't tell Burger Biggie about my plan, but I think they knew an older gentleman like myself was not committed to a career in burger flipping.

My next move was to lease a one-bedroom apartment over a grocery store. As expected, it did not have a wood-burning fireplace. But it did have a nice view of the highway. It had a monthly rent that started out reasonable, but jumped to ridiculous during ski season. It was not within walking distance of the ski lift, unless you were into hiking in full ski regalia. However, it was on the bus line – and I wouldn't have to worry about driving in the snow to get groceries.

All and all, while the job and the accommodations were a bit south of satisfactory, at least I had a toehold from which I could shop for something better. I moved in and went to work.

As a social entrée, Burger Biggie was a flop. Most of the staff – maybe all – were way under thirty. For the time being, though, it was OK. And at the end of the day we got to split all the leftover burgers and fries. Yum. To spin it positive, since the assistant manager trainee had to work the late shift, I had a great opportunity to scout around for good places to hike and bike during the day. It didn't much matter that I didn't get off until midnight. There wasn't anybody around anyway.

If I had been selling it, I would have described my apartment as cozy. But even with a secondhand TV and a used bike, it was fine for one person. Everything worked. At first there was a problem with Rocky Mountain rats. Yes, it seems that the rats liked to hang out at my place until the grocery store closed for the night. However, after a fierce battle, I was successful in driving them out – into adjoining apartments, I suppose. In any case, they left me alone.

For a month and a half, I hiked, biked, and flipped

burgers. On my night off, I lurked through mostly empty bars in the village and bitched about the lack of women to an understanding twenty-one-year-old co-worker. He explained in broken English that "thems locals doan go there, man," and suggested a couple of places down valley. Unfortunately, an older white guy in a bar of young Hispanics didn't work out very well. I honed my hiking and biking skills.

Finally, blessedly, the hotel personnel woman called. Could I come in the next Saturday for my orientation?

With apologies, I gave notice to Burger Biggie. I thought it was a bit short, but oddly, the manager was not unhappy with my abrupt departure. He said most people just left after a payday and never came back; he added that I could have my job back anytime. I bid a fond farewell, in Spanish, to my co-workers, and left the burger business forever, I hoped.

After spending thirty-odd years as a suit-and-tie semi-professional, it was good to get back to a place where people wore something other than blue jeans and t-shirts to work. Putting my best foot forward, I showed up at the hotel in a collared shirt and slacks. The personnel lady seemed a little surprised to see me. I don't think she had checked the age part on my employment application. Nonetheless, she showed me around, explained my duties, and walked me through the mass of papers I had to sign in order to work for the hotel. In the process, when my gaze wandered to an attractive woman in the hotel lobby, she noted that one of the hotel's "no-nos" was fraternizing with guests. It was a firing offense, she emphasized. I wondered if there was a list of other no-nos somewhere that I needed to read.

Most of my new co-workers were twenty-somethings, but the personnel lady – who turned out to be my boss – was a reasonable distance from my age. She, however, was either a lesbian, just didn't like me, or felt the need to impress upon me that she was management and I wasn't. Not even a hint of a smile for my best cute remarks.

As it turned out, the "relief desk clerk" was a lot more full-time than part-time. That was OK with me. I enjoyed learning the hotel business and looked forward to coming to work each day. I guess old habits die hard.

About a month had passed when I got a note saying the personnel lady wanted to see me. Although I couldn't think of anything I had done wrong – certainly no fraternization – these kinds of summonses have a way of not being good news.

"Ms. Voertman," I said as I entered her office. "You wanted to see me?"

"Have a seat," she said, adding, "You can call me Lindsey."

This might not be so bad after all, I thought, even though she sat silently, giving me a puzzled look. Finally she asked "Why are you here?"

My first impulse was to say "Because you wanted to see me," but I figured that was a little too sarcastic. Instead, I played for time. "What do you mean?"

"What I mean is that you've been here a month and, not counting the manager, you're the best employee we have. Never call in sick on pretty days. Always on time. Happy to work late. Don't make many mistakes. Play by the rules. And you're an older man with a college degree and excellent references. Why would you come to Vail and work in a hotel?"

I paused, wondering if I should give her the long answer or something else. I opted for true, but vague. "Change."

She continued to peer at me as if the real answer might appear on my forehead. Then she continued. "I know asking people around here 'How long do you intend to work here?' is like whistling in the dark. So I'll skip that and cut to the chase. I... We," she corrected, "like you. The manager and I think you'd work out well as the lead desk clerk. It would come with a raise, of course." She paused again. "In the real world, I wouldn't have to ask this, but would you be interested?"

She was dead-on with that. I almost laughed. *Would I be interested? Are you crazy?* But then it was my turn to hesitate. *Why exactly was I here?* I mused.

"How much time would I get off?" I answered.

At that she blinked. "I guess you're not an alien, after all."

She assured me that the hotel understood the work-force in a resort. I'd have ample time to pursue my outside interests and, if things worked out, I could stay on between seasons. I had been a little concerned about what I'd do between the summer and the winter seasons, with the specter of Burger Biggie lurking on the edges of my consciousness. I accepted her offer and things got even better.

One day Lindsey and I chanced to leave work at the same time. I smiled and waved. She stopped me.

"I've noticed you ride a bike to work. Is that what you do for fun?" she said.

Fighting my every instinct to jump on that one, I answered, "That and hike. River stuff is a bit much for me."

Apparently it was best that I had restrained myself. She went on to explain that she and a few other people met once a week for a bike ride, and wondered if I'd like to join them.

Yes! I thought. I had finally pierced the social veil. (No pun intended.)

"We meet on Wednesday mornings for breakfast, then ride for however long it takes," she said.

"Sounds like fun to me, but I'm not a pro-caliber rider."

She explained that the group wasn't all pro athletes, either. "We just like to ride the roads around here."

Thinking back, that should have been the clue. There were maybe two rides around the valley that weren't straight up. But I was thinking about finally getting to meet some people and, besides that, I had been riding the area for a couple of months and felt I was a pretty good biker.

"OK, then. Tomorrow at eight o'clock at the breakfast diner in Minturn," she concluded.

We parted with a smile. I was looking forward to it.

Minturn, Colorado. July. 8 AM. 47°. It's cold. Maybe my work hours, or maybe my normal mode of dress hadn't prepared me for this. A short-sleeved bike shirt and bike shorts were not quite enough at this hour. Almost everybody else, except some guy who looked like a fugitive from *Grizzly Adams*, was wearing long pants and jackets.

"Well, hi. I'm glad you made it." It was Lindsey surveying me. "You gonna be warm enough?"

"Sure," I lied. "Up north we're used to this kind of weather. Where are we headed?"

"Leadville." She looked slightly puzzled. "I think. David's our leader for the day. I think that's what he said."

Leadville?! I thought. *That's thirty miles and two mountain passes from here.* What I said was "Great" – perhaps a little forlornly.

Lindsey apparently picked up on my misgivings. "Oh, we don't ride very fast. We'll get there, relax over lunch, and then ride back this afternoon."

Ride back. Oh my God. I hadn't considered that. I

showed my teeth in a weak attempt at a smile.

The good news was that after five minutes up Battle Mountain, cold was no longer a problem. That, and I got to see an old abandoned mining town as I rode by very, very slowly. The road down was, of course, a lot easier – but the distance between me and the nothingness I could see off the side of the road kind of took the fun out of it. Due to the speed of my ascent and my death-grip on the hand brakes during the descent, by the time I crossed a big old green bridge at the bottom, I was dead last. In fact I could no longer see any other riders.

I wasn't very tired, though. Perhaps the fear of falling off a cliff on a bicycle does that. But the road gentled out and I felt good riding along beside a clear-running river on the way to the next climb. This one wasn't as bad as Battle Mountain – mostly because there were a lot of trees blocking the void. But it still seemed pretty much up all the way to Leadville.

Nobody had told me where we were eating lunch, but I really didn't care. In fact, I kind of hoped I wouldn't find them. Maybe then I could catch a ride in some pickup truck back to Minturn. No such luck. It was hard to miss twenty bicycles jammed around a small café.

The final ride into Leadville had taken all of whatever I had left. But I smiled and tried to stand up straight as I entered the café, thinking a little food and some rest might perk me up. However, as I walked in, my group was walking out.

"Hey," said Lindsey. "I thought we lost you. Just getting here?"

As I collapsed on a barstool, I mumbled something about a wrong turn. She explained that the group was going to get some ice cream, and I had plenty of time to eat before they started back.

These people must eat like starved wolves, I thought. Into my second bite of hamburger, I noticed the group getting cranked for the return trip.

"You about ready?" Lindsey said, checking on me before they left.

I explained that I'd be a couple of minutes, but they shouldn't wait. I'd catch up with them when I finished my food. That worked out for everybody. They weren't thinking about waiting, and I wasn't even considering gobbling my hamburger so I could jump back on a bicycle. I smiled. She left. I slumped on the bar.

It seemed logical that the trip back to Minturn would be a lot like the trip to Leadville – just backwards. But it turned out that, while I was eating, the Colorado Department of Transportation had somehow managed to take the "down" out of the trip back to Battle Mountain. And about the time I got to the old green bridge, the traditional afternoon thunderstorm hit. As is almost always the case, it didn't last very long, but now I was wet and cold as well as totally exhausted. In a way, that was good. My physical state kept my mind off the slick road on the steep descent around hairpin curves on the back side of the mountain. Finally getting home, I flopped down on the floor and knew nothing more until the alarm from my bedroom roused me for work.

As I entered the hotel, I forced myself to walk like a normal person. That is, I abandoned the Frankenstein-like lurching shuffle dictated by every muscle in my body painfully fighting movement.

Lindsey greeted me with a friendly smile and said "What happened to you? I waited for a while, but...."

"Yeah, I know," I explained. "I got caught in the rain."

"Rain?" She paused. "Oh. We missed it. Boy, I hate it

when it rains on me."

For the rest of the summer, I dodged most of the invitations to join the group for rides. At first I had rationalized that it was the ten to fifteen years these people had on me that accounted for my inability to keep up. Then I realized that there were five or so people in the bike group who were older than I was. I kept riding, though, at my own pace. It was better that way.

The hotel kept me on for the shoulder season and none of my co-workers – including Lindsey – could understand why I seemed so happy when there were no longer any long rides to go on. I even found a nice lady or two to share nonathletic time with.

In early December the snow began to fall, and fall, and fall. It was great for a skier. If there's anyplace in the world with better skiing of all varieties than the Vail Valley, I'm not aware of it. If it was daylight and I wasn't working, I was on the mountain.

Then one day, once again I happened to leave work with Lindsey. "Hey," she said, "I see you're a skier."

I nodded enthusiastically.

"Well, there's a group of us who get together on Wednesdays in Vail to ski."

If that sounds vaguely familiar, it is. It's downright identical – except for the snow and spoked wheels. Although wisdom is transitory, apparently stupidity is forever. I bought in again.

The skiing immediately began with a gut-wrenching push off a cornice that should have been called Instant Death, progressed into the trees and through the moguls, and into moguls covered with trees. Where there was nothing to leap off or cut in between, we went fast – very fast. I was, of course, last, and if you've ever occupied that position in a ski group, you know the drill. The group rests while they wait for you, and when you finally catch up, huffing and puffing, legs burning, they say "OK. He's here. Let's go."

At some point we all stopped for a very brief lunch, then started in again for round two. Sometime early into this second round, I arrived disguised as a snowball on a catwalk at the bottom of some unnamed glade. Discovering that there was no one around from my group, I was elated. Apparently I had taken a wrong tumble and ended up alone. I could now snowplow slowly down the catwalk and go home gracefully. There was no hope of hooking up with the group again, and after dragging me all over the mountain most of the day, I was confident they would not wait for me long.

Following the pattern I had set in summer, I continued to ski mostly by myself while devising myriad excuses for being unavailable on Wednesdays. Having worked for the hotel for one full season and most of another, not counting Lindsey and the manager, I was senior man on the job. And that was fine. I continued to enjoy learning how hotels work.

On the other hand, even with snowshoeing, what could have been a relatively relaxed activity turned into a physical challenge. All of the locals seemed bound and determined to push everything they did to the max. I became convinced that all these people had a death wish.

Furthermore, it was always cold – not just a good nip in the air, but mind-numbing, breath-freezing, die-if-you-stay-out-too-long cold. Up in the morning – cold. Go outside – cold. Stay inside – cold. Everywhere all the time – cold. And the lack of humidity meant slathering your body with goo or having your skin crinkle, crack, and fall off. Of course, there was the snow. By the end of the season, my car was a giant dirty snowball. That's because driving in the stuff was an accident crapshoot. The car hadn't moved in months.

Then, of course, there was the resort syndrome. That's what locals contract when continually exposed to party-hardy tourists. For some reason, perhaps overexposure, the locals begin to believe that, in addition to working all day and skiing when they're not working, they must also party all night like the tourists. Otherwise cheerful locals become irritable and short with everybody. Something in the skin tone is grayish. But mostly it's the eyes. They become dull and lifeless. Finally comes the full-blown flame-out and departure.

Maybe because of my age, I wasn't quite as susceptible as my younger brethren, but still I recognized the symptoms in myself and withdrew. Then my apartment began to shrink. To split time between work and a small hovel was not why I came to Colorado. I had to do something.

"Good morning," I said when Lindsey reported for work. "Can we talk?"

Once seated in her office, I explained the problem and asked if it would be possible to transfer to another hotel in the chain somewhere in the real world. I was moderately surprised when she not only seemed to understand, but also said she'd be happy to facilitate the transfer.

"I've worked at this hotel for a long time and, believe me, this isn't the first time this has happened. Under the glitz, it's a hard life. Some people can adjust; some can't. It's like the altitude. I think it's in the genes."

I didn't say "And it helps if you're twenty-something." I just nodded.

"So... what should I put as the reason for the transfer request?"

"This is no country for old wusses." I smiled.

She smiled back.

CHANGE OF LIFE

Bobby Bertelli and I went to high school together in Dallas. But when I headed out for the "halls of ivy," Bobby went to work in his father's garage – that's "garage" as in where you go to get your car fixed. While Bobby was busy learning the car-fixing business, I was busy preparing for a grand career in law that would lead to faraway places and an excellent income. In fact it was many, many years after high school that I again encountered Bobby.

One of the first things I learned after retirement to my old hometown was that when my car didn't work, I didn't have the option of trading it back to the law firm for a new one. That nugget of wisdom was almost immediately followed by the realization that a grand career in law does not prepare one to deal with the intricacies of automotive repair. What I vaguely remembered being under the hood of a '63 Chevy had been replaced with a cacophony of gismos and doodads that cannot be described in English. That was when I remembered Bobby.

Bobby's dad's place had been in a seedy part of Dallas where you could pick up a hooker while you waited to have your car fixed. Foolishly – and there is no fool like an old fool – I assumed that Bobby would still be there, so I drove my wounded vehicle to the old garage. Ha.

Not only was Bertelli's Garage no longer there, the whole area was no longer there. Instead there was a high-rise condominium surrounded by an upscale shopping mall. No rundown buildings. No hookers – at least, no hookers that looked like I remembered them. Fortunately, though, the helpful doorman at the high-rise was a long-time local and he explained that Bertelli's Garage had moved north. Instead of Bertelli's Garage, it was now Import Maintenance of Greater Dallas, specializing in Mercedes and Lexus. The doorman gave me directions, and having no other immediate alternative, off to the north I went.

Well, if Bobby's old neighborhood had surprised me, the trip north was a major cognitive adjustment. In my absence, the Dallas Metroplex had apparently gobbled up all the nice little towns between Dallas and the Oklahoma border – now it was one long stretch of very nice housing developments and shopping malls. After an hour or so, sure enough, there was Import Maintenance – a sprawling concrete-and-glass affair sporting the biggest American flag I had ever seen.

At that point, I should have turned around and gone home, but I wasn't sure I knew where home was from here. And I was definitely concerned that my car wouldn't make it – wherever it was. So instead of wedging my slightly aging American model into a mass of Lexi and Mercedi, I elected to park and see if I could find Bobby.

Approaching what looked like the garage area, I was stopped by a big orange sign: "MAINTENANCE AREA. STAFF <u>ONLY</u>. ENTER THROUGH LOBBY." *Hmm*, I thought, but after living a life of following instructions, I did as directed.

The lobby was no small dusty room crammed with old files and monitored by an aging employee at an old cash register. More like a grand ballroom featuring a variety of refreshments and comfy chairs for waiting customers. In the center was a raised and rounded desk that said "Concierge." *A bit over the top*, I was thinking as I approached.

"Can we be of service to you?" A perky young lady who could have doubled as a cheerleader for Neiman-Marcus casual wear beamed at me.

I explained that I wanted to see Bobby Bertelli.

"Oh," she said. "Do you have an appointment?"

Saying "No," I watched Susie-Q's smile flatten. "But I'm an old friend." I thought I recovered nicely.

The smile returned. "Let me check. Can I give his secretary your name?"

I gave it to her.

"Please have a seat." She gestured toward the comfy chairs. "And please help yourself to the refreshments."

After what appeared to be intense negotiations with the unseen secretary, Susie-Q smiled again in my direction. "It shouldn't be very long. Is there anything I can get you?"

"Very long" is apparently a relative term. As I sipped my third latte and watched the old second hand crawl around, I began weighing the merits of waiting forever or trying to drive my car anywhere. Lost in mental debate, I was surprised when Susie-Q materialized in front of me.

"Mr. Bertelli will see you now. Just follow me," she chirped.

Across the grand ballroom, down a long hall to large wooden double doors we went. Gently opening the door, as one might when entering a cathedral, we crept in. This was just the secretary's office.

Susie-Q introduced me to Tiffany, the secretary. If Susie-Q was a cheerleader, Tiffany was a runway model. "Please be seated," she purred. "Mr. Bertelli will be right with you. Would you like some coffee while you wait?"

After about thirty more minutes, something buzzed on Tiffany's desk and she said, "Mr. Bertelli will see you now. Please walk this way." As Tiffany moved toward the boss's door, the old joke came back. I thought, but didn't say, *I couldn't walk that way in a million years.* Tiffany probably wouldn't appreciate the humor.

"Hey," said Bobby, rising in the distance from behind an incredible expanse of desk. "How you been?" Bobby did not look like Bobby. Bobby looked like Danny DeVito emerging from a shopping trip at Armani. "Long time, heh? What's going on? What's on your mind?" Mirroring that progression of greetings, Bobby's bright smile gradually disappeared.

It occurred to me that, considering the number of years since our last meeting, Bobby probably thought I was here to borrow money or sell him something. I explained my presence.

Bobby's smile returned at medium brightness. "Well, you know we really don't do much with American cars. I don't mean we couldn't, but it'd cost a lot more." Bobby raised his eyebrows.

I shrugged.

"But, hey. You know cars are kinda like people. The older they get, the more things go wrong with 'em. First, your tires wear out. Then something more essential – something under the hood. Then it's just one thing going wrong after another. You can rebuild the car, but it's never gonna be like it used to be. It gets pretty expensive and your insurance isn't gonna pay for it." He moved his head slowly, as if to say "Sad but true." He paused. "Say, why don't I put you in a new car?"

I shrugged again, weighing the pros and cons.

"If… you know, money is the problem, we got a great

pre-owned lot. Driven by little ol' ladies, and they come with a damn good warranty." He chuckled.

I felt fairly sure that last little bit about money was the hook in this part of the world. Nobody in North Dallas wanted to admit that money might be a problem.

"Bobby, it's not the money. This is a second car. Something to putz around in. I don't need a nice new Mercedes – or even a pre-owned Lexus – to drive to the store and back."

Bobby gave me the "Oh?" look and I could see the wheels turning. *Does he really live in Dallas?*

After that, the silence got awkward. Bobby glanced at his watch, and I took the cue. We, of course, shook hands and exchanged pleasantries. He even suggested we get together some time to talk about old times. And that was that. Tiffany smiled at me as I left. Susie-Q didn't notice.

Driving in the direction I thought was toward home, I had an odd feeling – kind of let down. It sure wasn't that Bobby hadn't done well with his life. Clearly he had. I guess the feeling was a bit of remorse because the Bobby I had known was gone. I suppose I had expected to find him under the hood of a car covered in grease and surrounded by the remnants of Bertelli's Garage.

I had changed. Why did I think the rest of the world wouldn't? I suppose it's a foundation problem. Somewhere in the back of everybody's mind, there must be an assumption that the parts and pieces that supported your development are permanent. The foundation of your own growth should remain stable, because if it doesn't – like the crumbling of the foundation of a house – the integrity of the structure is threatened.

Nothing is certain but death and taxes, and the only thing constant is change, I mused. Perhaps that's the basis of Thomas Wolfe's novel *You Can't Go Home Again*.

I wondered if Thomas also meant that your car might not make it, as something thumped under the hood.

WITNESS THE CIRCLE

Once upon a time in the kingdom of youth, he recalled the overwhelming, all-engulfing force of love. He was
twenty-five. She was twenty-one. They had chanced to meet
while moving between classes at the university. She had
dropped her books. He had reached to help her. The inci-
dental touch was a bolt of cosmic lightning. How silly they
must have looked – standing, staring, caught in the primal
grip of an ancient magic experienced as if totally fresh and
new. The unquenchable lust that followed, the bond that de-
fied separation for even a day, was baffling but unquestioned.

Then the waning tide of complete infatuation left a
less dazzling, less encompassing passion, but still as strong...
just different. Of course, they married. How he still loved his

wife.

These were the thoughts that reintegrated in his mind's eye, but mostly in his heart, as he fingered the beige embossed envelope addressed to him and his wife, soul mate, one and only love. He knew what was in the envelope. It had been well settled months before. Somehow, though, it was this envelope that made the act concrete, real, and capable of evoking such strong memories.

He didn't need to remove the delicate lace-like paper that announced he and his wife and some other guy and his wife were requesting the honor of someone's presence at the wedding of his son and their daughter in three months' time. He had seen the invitation already. In fact, his wife helped pick it out.

He supposed (hoped) that Junior and Sweetie Pie felt the way he and his wife had felt so long ago. What had he read recently? The divorce rate was now over fifty percent. He figured he could get almost the same odds in Vegas putting his money on red. When presented with the sizable cost of the wedding, he managed not to gag. He had also managed to restrain himself from making them an alternate proposition: "Elope, and if you make it five years, I'll give you a check in the amount I would have spent on the wedding."

For better or worse, to use a fitting term, this was his attitude as the big day approached. Other than in his own love life, he had always been a pragmatist. What's the risk? What's the return? What are the odds of success? Don't bet on a long shot. Only if Junior and Sweetie Pie managed to make it as long as he had – with just one woman and no slipping around – would the investment be worth it.

But that was not the way the handsome young couple saw things. Theirs was a union made in heaven and destined by deity. *And why is that?* he wondered. *Because that's what they thought. Nuts! Why can't they just live together like the rest of their morally deficient generation, and see how it works out?*

The bride's parents, Ralph and Alice – not their real names, but he couldn't remember their real names – seemed OK, but he had nothing in common with either of them, and they were as foolishly optimistic as the happy couple. He kept thinking, *What sort of people buy into this kind of semi-adolescent, pie-in-the-sky delusion? People who want to stop supporting a daughter? Or maybe it was because they were from California? People out there think differently.*

Even if he was wrong, and he hoped he was, there

were other things that bothered him about the whole proce-dure. For one, he had to wear a tuxedo to the wedding. *Why is that?* he asked himself. *All I have to do is walk in and sit down. I can do that in a nice suit. Nobody cares what I'm wearing. But that's the way the bride and groom want it. So now I have to rent a tuxedo, get it fitted, pick it up, take it back. For cryin' in a barrel. Is there any way I can spend more time and money?*

Actually, yes, he answered his own mental question. *Engagement parties, wedding showers, rehearsal dinner, reception, day-after brunch. And that's just the events I have to go to. There's also the bachelor party and the bachelorette party. These people think this is Mardi Gras.*

Although painful, time was swift. Sitting in the church, in his tuxedo, he decided, now that he was halfway through it, the preliminaries hadn't been so bad.

The rehearsal had gone quickly and, as he'd suspect-ed, he really didn't have to do anything but walk in and sit down. The following dinner had been good. There was a choice of entrées and it was so noisy, he couldn't hear – he could sit quietly and eat. The bill was steep, but they took plastic. It would be a month before he felt the pain. Plus he got frequent flyer points.

He didn't know firsthand about the bachelor parties. From the rumors, it would be luck if the wedding party was still alive and showed up at the wedding.

And now the music began. Sure enough, all the bridesmaids and groomsmen showed up. He counted them to make sure. Then the tittering hush and *dum dum de dum* pulsed from the organ somewhere in the back of the church.

Up front stood his boy – smiling, waiting, a look of genuine anticipation. He remembered that look. He had seen it on many Christmas mornings. *How could that little boy of many, many years ago have become this handsome, self-assured man? Where had the time gone?*

And, finally, the bride. She was truly radiant – even if she *was* escorted by what's-his-name.

The vows they repeated clearly and with feeling. It seemed they genuinely meant that their love should prevail until "death do us part." The symbolic rings were exchanged.

The minister, of course, had to make a pitch for his church, but otherwise, he stayed on point for the big finale: "Now I pronounce you man and wife."

He had not really thought about his reaction to the ceremony – how he would really be affected. He was embarrassed by the overflow of emotion. He prayed for the first time in a long time that the newly formed couple would be… what? Happy? No – too light. He wished for them with all his heart the same love he had found with the woman who now clutched his hand.

He had not dreamed that this beginning would provide some sort of closure for him. In a world where any crazy thing could and did happen daily, it was good to see the circle of things complete.

Now. Back to the business of life.

REBOOTING FATE

RE: Old Friend   May 6, 2009 10:26:01 AM CDT
From: William.J.Boston@apl.com
    To: Pamela_Jackson@bdr.com

If you're the same Pamela Jackson who graduated from State in '68, or thereabouts, please respond. I found your e-mail address in an old alumni address book. Long time no see. Willie Boston

RE: Old Friend   May 6, 2009 11:39:37 PM MDT
From: Pamshome@dmal.net
    To: William.J.Boston@apl.com

Wild Willie? Wow! I'm lucky you got me. I'm in the process of dropping my old e-mail address. This is my new one.

How long has it been? I haven't seen you since the day we didn't show up for graduation. What have you been up to? Pam

RE: Old Friend   May 7, 2009 11:30:05 PM CDT
From: William.J.Boston@apl.com
   To: Pamshome@dmal.net

Pamarama. We had some times, didn't we?

Since last I saw you, I've had three wives, six children, and a bunch of jobs. The good news is they were all good (except the wives, of course) and I moved up the corporate ladder. I don't think I was meant for marriage. But the kids are great. One's a doctor, two are lawyers, two are "life engineers" (housewives), and one is in between things. That's three girls and three boys. So far no grandchildren, but that's OK. The kids all seem pretty happy and none of them are in prison.

Hit the magic number last year, and MEGACO showed their indispensable Senior Marketing Vice President the door. But that works well for me. There're some things I never had time to do, and my parachute really was made of gold after all. I'm still pretty healthy, so now I'm off to see the world from a different angle.

What's the Gypsy Queen of Tarlton Hall been up to for... a

lot of years? Take care and keep in contact. WWB

RE: Old Friend   May 8, 2009 7:25:21 PM MDT
From: Pamshome@dmal.net
   To: William.J.Boston@apl.com

Three wives, huh? Some people never learn... or change.

Do you remember Jason Billingsly, III? He was a Sig Ep at State. I didn't know him well in college. Had some classes together. His folks had a lot of money. Well, Jason was spouse number only. We ran into each other three or four years after college. Fell hopelessly in love and married. After five wonderful years, Jason was taken. He hung an edge doing a ski-bump run and slid into the trees.

I'm sure I'll never quite get over it, but I'm OK now. It's amazing what a little time in the funny farm and a great life will do.

Before Jason, I flew for Delta. That lasted almost three years before the excitement wore off. In the meantime, I'd moved to Colorado. About the time I quit, I found Jason. He was a ski instructor in Vail. Being a ski bum seemed the right thing to do. And looking back, I wouldn't do it otherwise. I got gut-hooked on the whole Rocky Mountain thing. Still love it. Never did get to use that degree in psychology.

Lucky for me Jason came into my life in the first place, but he also left me financially comfortable with a nice little place in the mountains. I guess it's unfortunate that Jason and I never had kids. But then I've never been a mother kinda chick. You think?

I really don't need to work, but a part-time job keeps me in touch with what's going on in the valley, and gives me plenty of me-time. This season, I got a job as a resort guide, and it starts first thing early early in the morning. So I better go. Take care. Keep in touch – really. Pam

RE: Old Friend   May 9, 2009 5:15:00 PM CDT
From: William.J.Boston@apl.com
   To: Pamshome@dmal.net

Mother? That wouldn't have been my guess. If anyone had asked, I'd have put you pretty much where you are. Class of '68: Girl most likely to be a hippie ski bum.

I guess it's been a long time, but I'm still sorry to hear about Jason. And you're right, I never knew him very well. Didn't he drive a red Corvette convertible in college?

You sound like you've had an exciting life. Mine has been pretty much by the business-major career guidebook. Signed on as an accountant at a big company right out of college.

Met Wife One at a singles bar after work. Married. Had two kids. Moved up changing jobs to sales. Somehow lost Wife One on the road. Wife Two was DOB (daughter of boss). Married and had two more kids. Moved up to sales manager. After a while, it got real old being married to Daddy's Little Princess. The job involved a lot of travel and gave me MOM – the means and opportunity. I guess I always had the motive. Princess divorced me. Lost that job, but landed on my feet at a better company as VP of Marketing. Wife Three had one kid when we met, and we had a second one. That union died from lack of interest when the kids left. What can I say? I'm maritally unstable, but I keep climbing the ladder.

On the other hand, if you're looking for a salesman or someone to party with, I'm your guy. I guess what I learned in college stuck with me.

Do you remember Chip McCleary? We called him Dex because he always had some little exam helpers to sell? I went to Chip's funeral last week. We were pretty close in college and I just happened to read his obit in the newspaper. Talked to his sister Laurie and the whole thing was pretty sad. It seems that when you went off to fly and I went off to sell, Chip went off to be a criminal. Laurie said Chip had been in trouble ever since he left college. Went to prison three times – in more years than he was out. She said he had just gotten out again a couple of months ago. Tried to stick up a drive-in grocery and the clerk blew him away. He was a sharp guy in college. Could have been anything he wanted to be. Sad.

Hey, there's a high note to end on. Tell me, how'd the first day on the job go? WW

RE: Old Friend   May 11, 2009 12:01:40 PM MDT
From: Pamshome@dmal.net
   To: William.J.Boston@apl.com

Some things never change in this valley. My new boss is an asshole… apparently a horny asshole. I guess you could say he's a very touchy person – the old mountain goat. He's one of those guys who thinks women are good for only one thing. You'd think he'd be too busy with making his reservations at the old folks home to be chasing women my age. The good news is there's no good reason to see much of him after to-day. I think between dodging hits, I learned all I need to know about being a resort guide – smile and tell 'em where the best restaurant is.

But despite it all, it was a beautiful day here today – at least if you kept looking up. It's still spring and that means it's mud season. The snow continues to melt, revealing an amazing variety of stuff dropped by skiers and, of course, mud. It's still a bit chilly unless you stop in the shade; then it's cold. But the locals think it's summer. After lots of snow and sub-zero temps, shorts and t-shirts are the order of the day. Who can blame 'em? All snow and no heat make Jackie… crazy. Or something like that. I'd send you a picture, but I'm not exactly a techie.

I do remember Chip. That's too bad. I liked him a lot. I guess you just never know.

I ran into Judy Starns awhile back. She's not dead or anything, but she seems to be broke. I don't know if you remember, but she graduated magna cum laude "laude I'm smart." Her degree was in finance. Became a real hotdog stockbroker/investor in New York. Used to come through here in her private jet. What you might call a snow queen for a lot of reasons.

She told me the whole "masters of the universe" lifestyle went to her head. Invested all her money in a sleeper stock that couldn't help but take off. Stock went south instead and she lost everything. She had to borrow enough money to buy a used car to drive to California to move in with her only son. I told her she could stay with me for a while, but she declined. Actually, I'm glad. Seems like down people can bring you down a lot easier than you can bring them up. If Judy's mood goes any further down, I wouldn't give you much for her chances of living long.

What is the deal? That's twice we've ended on a bad note. Hope this isn't a trend. Tell me something good. Pam

RE: Old Friend   May 12, 2009 3:16:29 PM CDT
From: William.J.Boston@apl.com
   To: Pamshome@dmal.net

I know what you mean about being a techie. I do real well to
send and receive e-mail, but that's about it. I guess it shows
my age when I say I miss the printed word. And what in the
world is a tweeter?

I remember Judy. She was good looking as well as smart. Absolutely had it all. Too bad.

Sometimes I wonder why I've done as well as I have. I don't
think anybody would have predicted it. Wild partier. Gentleman's "C." Somewhere just above last in our class. What I
really wonder is why I'm here at all. Do you remember some
of the stuff we used to do?

I used to believe that God protected drunks and little kids,
but I'm not sure that He protects little kids anymore. Can't
pick up a newspaper without seeing where some youngster
got killed.

What do you do for fun up there in God's country? (I'm trying to make a nice save from ending on a sour note.) Do you
still like to party hardy?

I try, but I like to exercise, too. It's a good thing. Otherwise
I'd be fatter than I already am. I like to bike and walk on the

beach… which segues nicely into the weather.

I think it's already summer down here. I don't see how it can get much hotter or much more humid. But it's not bad for biking. Take care and watch out for the boss. WW

RE: Old Friend   May 13, 2009 9:00:04 PM MDT
From: Pamshome@dmal.net
    To: William.J.Boston@apl.com

The old party-down routine is a thing of the past. Of course, my long-time companion, Mr. Cigarette, is no longer on the scene. Only kids and the chronically habituated smoke now. (Hope you don't.) I'm a real clean liver – by default, but I'll take credit for it anyway.

I pretty much go with the season for exercise. Winter – ski and snowshoe. Summer – bike and hike. In between, try to be elsewhere. Biking up here is a little bit different. You can only go two ways, up or down. Unless you like communing with cars.

I know what you mean about wondering how we managed to do so well. Do you believe in God?

I'll leave it on that metaphysical note. Gotta go. Someone's knocking. Take care. Pam

RE: Old Friend   May 14, 2009 10:25:59 PM CDT
From: William.J.Boston@apl.com
  To: Pamshome@dmal.net

To answer your questions directly, no, I don't smoke, and yes, I believe in God. I'm not sure I know exactly what He does, though. I mean when you look around and see the things that happen, you gotta wonder why. But maybe more to the point, why me?

I don't fancy myself a particularly good person. I'm not brighter, stronger, faster, or better looking than a lot of folks. Yet other people die, have injuries, go broke, lose loved ones, and have any number of terrible things happen to them – and I don't. Why not?

The idea that this is random luck tends to be terrifying. If God's watching me, why wasn't He watching those other people? How many people have you known personally who fall into the category of hard luck cases? Or of being dead? Why not you? I don't think either of us has lived our life cloistered in cotton and out of harm's way.

Maybe that's the beer talking. I think I'll call it a night. Take care. WW

RE: Old Friend   May 15, 2009 9:30:50 PM MDT
From: Pamshome@dmal.net
  To: William.J.Boston@apl.com

You know what I think about? All those people in Africa or
Bangladesh or any number of countries who seem to die or
be murdered by the tens of thousands or who are enslaved or
who live under almost sub-human conditions. Why exactly is
it that we don't? Because some trick of fate caused us to be
born in this country and in this time period?

And that's just step one. Like you say, after the incredible
luck of being born in the United States, then somehow you
dodge the issues of poverty, disease, ignorance, abnormality,
criminal involvement, mental illness, early death, and on and
on. How come that is?

Why am I sitting here in Vail, Colorado, at age sixty-
something with plenty of money and in good health while,
even in this country, people just like me are dying at an early
age? How many times in my life could I have taken the wrong
turn and ended up dead or in prison? And you don't really
have to take the wrong turn. You can be riding along following all the rules in your car when a boulder tumbles down the
mountain and squashes you. (At least, up here you can. It's
probably not a big problem where you live.:))

I don't think I'll think about this anymore. It's too freaky.
Take care. Pam

RE: Old Friend   May 16, 2009 11:30:00 PM CDT
From: William.J.Boston@apl.com
   To: Pamshome@dmal.net

Is this where we have another toke and make love? Oh, sorry.
That was a hundred years ago. You'd think we'd have gotten
all this straightened out by now.

But, seriously, I was thinking about adding Vail in the mud
season to my travel agenda. Whadaya think? Would that work
for you? Willie

THINGS NOT DONE

On the scale of beach bars that run from "yuppie bring your family" to "don't go in without a weapon," the Sandcrab Island Bar is somewhere near the latter end of the spectrum. It opens at precisely ten in the morning and closes when the barmaid or owner can persuade the locals to stagger on home. It is always dark – only lit by glowing neon liquor signs and a small penlight near the cash register. It always smells of stale beer and cigarette smoke. It always has at least one customer sitting at the bar nursing his or her drink of choice. It's a bar "where everybody knows your name" because it mostly attracts local islanders who are past the prime of life and on the final downhill run. It isn't that tourists and young folks aren't welcome; they just wouldn't like it.

The drinks are cheap and the beer is cold, but the owner makes ends meet due to the nature of his clientele. They don't stop in for just one drink and most are there every day of the year. Also, as far as anyone knows, the place hasn't been remodeled or upgraded in its thirty-year history – not counting sweeping out the sand and nailing back a few fixtures after a hurricane. Overhead expense is negligible.

In the twilight milieu of the Sandcrab, time is suspended. Day and night are indistinguishable and, with only the glow of beer signs, the age of the patrons is difficult to determine absent a very close inspection. And closely scrutinizing anything in the Sandcrab is a serious breach of protocol meriting a knot on the head or a well-placed slap and perhaps expulsion.

There is a jukebox filled with oldies with the volume turned low. Drinking and conversation are the entertainment. Only the owner feels compelled to occasionally put coins in the jukebox to make sure the thing still works. Likewise there is an antique television mounted on the wall in back of the bar. It is always on, but only made audible when the Weather Channel talks about a hurricane in the Gulf of Mexico.

*****

Outside the cool dark of the Sandcrab, on this particular day, it was August. The water temperature in the gulf was easily ninety degrees, which meant the air surrounding it was unbearable absent shade. Even the vacationers sought the protection of air-conditioned accommodations. Inside the Sandcrab, August was just another month. However, one did have to get there, and getting there meant fighting the melting heat. Perhaps that circumstance accounted for the lack of much talk in the Sandcrab.

Three of the locals were dispersed around the L-shaped bar silently nursing drinks and staring at vacant space, waiting for the drink or the surroundings or both to regenerate enough energy to speak... or order another drink.

Bark broke the silence with a noise somewhere between a cough and a laugh. "Bark" wasn't really the man's name. Last names were never offered or used. In the Sandcrab, the *nom de guerre* was either acquired by way of introduction or conferred by the group. In Bark's case, he came by his nickname as a rookie when he showed up wearing a t-shirt that read "Bark" and something about a dog that nobody paid any attention to.

This unexpected noise brought questioning looks

from the other two patrons. When Bark gave no explanation, Muff, the only female, spoke. "What's the problem, Bark? Forget that stuff's for drinkin', not inhalin'?"

"Naw," said Bark, "I was just thinkin' 'bout somethin'." He lapsed back into silence.

"Damn, Bark. Let us in on the big secret." TJ, the other male patron, had apparently recovered enough energy to be curious.

"Wellll…" Bark stretched the word while looking into the nonexistent distance and rubbing his chin whiskers. "It's kind of a funny thing to think about. Just popped into my mind."

Muff and TJ waited.

Muff finally said, "Come on, Bark. We're all friends here. Besides, if somebody don't say somethin', I may have to order another drink."

"Well, Lord forbid," mocked TJ.

Muff gave him a sour look.

"Alright. Y'all two don't squabble. I'll tell you." He paused for a drink. "How old do you think I am?"

At the Sandcrab, age was another taboo subject. So Muff and TJ were a little wary about answering.

"Heck, I don't know. Guess 'bout as old as I am." TJ neatly dodged the subject.

Muff just smiled and nodded.

"Well, I'll tell you. I'm seventy-two years old as of yesterday," Bark explained.

"Hey, happy birthday... late." Muff interrupted, tilting her glass in a toast.

Bark gave her a look that said, "You want me to tell this story or what?"

Muff shrugged.

"Like I was sayin' before somebody interrupted me." He glanced at Muff. "I'm seventy-two, and all my life I've been terrified of tornados. Of course, we don't get many on the beach, but when I lived in town, I was scared shitless — pardon my French, Muff — of the things. Come springtime, I'd get worried on cloudy days. Thunderstorms would have me lookin' over my shoulder. And if they issued a "watch" or "alert," I just plain couldn't function. Alert time was time to hit the sauce hard. I couldn't do anything. Couldn't concentrate on work, if I was at work. Hell, I couldn't concentrate if I wadn't at work. If they issued the alert at night, I couldn't sleep 'til the alert was over. I'm tellin' you, it's terrible." Bark stopped talking and took another drink. Just talking about it had him in a dither.

TJ nodded.

Muff sympathized, "Yeah, I guess it would be."

They waited.

When Bark didn't continue, after giving Muff a look, TJ said, "So… what's the point, Bark?"

"The point," Bark said, looking at his comrades like they were idiots, " is a tornado has never got near me."

Muff blinked.

TJ squinted his eyes.

"Don't y'all see? Seventy-two years of worrying for nothin'. April through September I've been sweatin' bullets ever' damn year and nothin'. Now I'm old enough so it don't matter much. What an incredible waste of time and energy." He paused, then made that noise again.

"I remember one time I was with a client – makin' a sale, you know. He was a general contractor and I met him in his trailer at the job site. I could see a big ol' black cloud out the window over his shoulder comin' our way. So I suggested we go on over to a buildin' he was buildin' and continue our discussion there. He asked me why we'd want to do such a thing, and I said somethin' silly like we might be more comfortable over there. He suggested I come back to see him some other time. And you know what? I was just happy as hell about that until the sky cleared up and I realized I'd blown the sale." Bark just shook his head looking into his drink. "Idn't that crazy? Seventy-two years and not even a close call. I've got half a mind to go find a storm and dare a tornado to get me."

"I wouldn't go that far, Bark," said TJ. "But I see what you mean."

Muff didn't seem to be listening to Bark. Clearly she was somewhere else. Then in the ensuing silence she blurted, "I know just what you mean." Her statement wasn't one of agreement or consolation, but an affirmative declaration that left little doubt she had a similar story.

Both men focused on her – waiting.

"OK, then," she said, knocking back the rest of her drink. "I'm not about to tell y'all how old I am, but for however long it's been, I've been scared of somebody breakin' into my house at night and doin' something terrible." She exhaled mightily as if just saying the words were a great relief.

"That's not so unusual. You're a lone woman – at

least as far as I know. There's a lot of crazy people out there and you just never know." TJ sympathized.

"Yeah well, there's lots of lone women out there. Wanna see somethin'?" She hesitated, making sure the bar-maid was still in the back room. When both men nodded, Muff withdrew a nickel-plated .38 revolver from her purse, raised her eyebrows at the men, then replaced it. "I'm not worried about being in this bar, but sometime I'm gonna have to go home. And walkin' into a dark house just scares me to death."

Both men shrugged like that was of no great moment.

"Hey." Bark spoke first. "That's not such a big deal. A woman by herself needs to be a little worried. What I mean is the threat is a lot more real than being sucked up by a tor-nado."

"That may be true," Muff continued, "but what you don't know is that the closer it gets to goin' home time, the more I worry... and the more I drink." She stopped and con-sidered. "It ought to be the other way 'round. I mean, if I get too drunk, I might shoot myself. But that's not the way it works and that ain't all. When I get home, I'll turn on all the lights in the house and search it thoroughly – I mean windows, doors, and closets. Then I'll lock up and turn on the alarm system. If I don't do that, I can't sleep. Lay awake all night listening for noises that shouldn't be there." Muff made a gesture with her hand signifying futility.

"You know, Muff, that's not so bad." TJ took a swallow before he continued. "I check my place every night, and I ain't got nothin' anyone might want." He leered at Muff for comic effect.

"TJ, you don't understand. It's like Bark said, this didn't just happen last week. It's been going on for years and years. I'm so sick of being scared..." She let the words trail off, then laughed. "But I'm not like Bark. I for sure ain't gonna go out and find me a nice rapist-murderer and get it over with." She paused again. "You think losin' a client is bad. How do you think I ended up with four no-good husbands? I think a lot of marryin' 'em was because I felt safer with 'em there at night. Then, of course, they were such stinkers, I figured bein' scared was better than bein' with 'em. But, like Bark said, what a waste of time. And nothin' has ever happened to me. Couple of guys got fresh, but that's the closest I ever came to havin' some nut hurt me." Finishing her story and realizing she was out of drink, Muff gave a nod to the barmaid.

Bark followed by giving the universal signal for another round.

After the drinks came, TJ became uncomfortably aware that Muff and Bark were looking expectantly at him. TJ chugalugged his drink and, looking a little blurry-eyed at his bar buddies, said "Germs."

Muff and Bark looked at TJ like he'd just asked if it was OK to go to the bathroom.

"Germs?" Bark said with a smile.

Muff was doing her best not to snigger.

"Yeah, germs. And it ain't funny."

In the past, Bark and Muff had noticed that TJ was a little persnickety, wiping things and using hand sanitizer, but they hadn't thought that was a bad thing. No telling what had been dragged into the Sandcrab, and for sure it hadn't ever been cleaned up. They said as much.

"If it was just that," TJ said, "it'd be one thing, but it's a hell of a lot more. You seen *Monk* on TV?" He waited for their affirmation. "Well, almost that bad." He reached into his front pockets and withdrew a package of handiwipes in one hand and hand sanitizer in the other. Setting those down, he pulled a handkerchief out of his back pocket. He then removed a surgical mask from inside his shirt, saying "Just in case."

"If I don't sterilize everything I might touch, I literally start to sweat, and then the bad part starts. It's like my imagination moves into high gear. I have thoughts about dying in ways so bad, I don't even want to talk about it. Have you ever thought about going out on a date with a problem like that? Ha. Girls aren't much interested in having their mouth rubbed with a handiwipe before you kiss 'em. And sex... well, you can see the problem. Havin' kids or grandkids would be a nightmare. All them dirty diapers and them puttin' their grubby little hands on me. I don't even like to be in the same room with kids. Too unpredictable. Never know when they might touch you. It's the constant worry that makes me crazy. Drinkin' helps, but the whole damn thing just drives me up a tree. It's been this way ever since I was a little kid."

Bark was laughing.

"And, yeah, I can see what Bark's laughin' about. I've never been sick a day in my life."

Jennifer, the barmaid, had probably been a showstopper as a young lady. She wasn't young anymore, but she still wore the getup. And with the lighting in the Sandcrab, she still looked pretty good. Having heard most of the conversation as she went in and out from behind the bar doing things that barmaids do, she decided to chime in. These were customers, but she probably knew them better and spent more time with them than anybody else in her life. She considered them friends. "I don't understand why y'all don't just stop doin' that stuff that bothers you."

That drew three condescending stares.

"Honey..." Muff spoke. "You just don't understand. We know these things are stupid. We know that they've kept us from really enjoying a lot of life. But that don't mean we can just stop doin' 'em. It don't work that way. We do that stuff because it keeps the level of fear from puttin' us in the loony bin." She looked at Bark and TJ.

They didn't disagree.

Jennifer thought about that for a minute. "You know, I hate to say this, but y'all ain't got that much longer. Almost all your life – a mighty long time – you been worryin' about this stuff happenin', and ain't nothin' happened. Don't you think if somethin' was gonna happen, it would've happened by now?"

An unusual silence followed until Bark broke it. "So... let's drink to things not done regardless of how and why they weren't."

They all raised their glasses except Jennifer. She just looked puzzled.